LOVE & RADIO

A GRIPPING STORY OF HEARTBREAK AND SUCCESS

Dee Dee Redding

ISBN: 979-8-9989483-0-5 (Paperback)
ISBN: 979-8-9989483-1-2 (Hardcover)
ISBN: 979-8-9989483-2-9 (eBook)

Book design by Dara Publishing LLC
Place of Publication: Macon, Georgia, 31220
Library of Congress: 2025910905
Printed in the United States of America.

Disclaimer: This is a work of fiction. Names, characters, businesses, places, events, and incidents are either the products of the author's imagination or are used in a fictitious manner. Any resemblance to actual persons, living or dead, or actual events is purely coincidental. The content of this book is intended for entertainment purposes only. While the story may explore real-life themes such as career challenges, family dynamics, personal growth, and romantic relationships, it is not intended as professional, legal, or psychological advice. The views and opinions expressed by the characters do not necessarily reflect those of the author or publisher.

Dedication

This book is dedicated to my brother O3.

You are gone but certainly not forgotten.

You inspired me to keep going no matter what,

and you made me realize that the love of family is priceless.

You are forever and always with me.

Miss you, O3.

TABLE OF CONTENTS

AUTHOR'S NOTE

When I first set out to write *Love and Radio*, I didn't just want to tell a story—I wanted to tell **your story**, my story, the story of every woman who has ever shouldered the weight of expectations while daring to dream bigger.

This book was born from a deep place in my heart—a space filled with questions about identity, legacy, and the delicate balance between chasing success and nurturing the parts of ourselves that often go unnoticed. Ann's journey is fictional, yes, but her struggles, her triumphs, her heartbreaks, and her resilience are real. They belong to so many women I've known, and maybe even to you.

If you've ever felt torn between duty and desire . . . If you've ever fought to be seen in a world that expects you to be everything to everyone . . . If you've ever stood at the intersection of love and loneliness, unsure of which way to go . . . This story is for you.

Love and Radio is a tribute to the women who choose themselves. It's a reminder that strength isn't about having it all figured out—it's about showing up, even when your voice shakes. It's about letting go of the pain you've normalized and stepping into the light of your own becoming.

Thank you for taking this journey with me. I hope Ann's story makes you feel seen, valued, and inspired to rewrite your own narrative with boldness and truth.

With all my heart,

Dee Dee Redding

CHAPTER 1

STATIC IN THE SIGNAL

"Hot 108: the hottest hip hop and R&B. It's your girl, Toni Foxx . . . keep it locked. I've got your chance to win tickets for the hottest concert to hit this area on October 17. More on that in a minute. Right now, check out this throwback on Hot 108."

It's nine a.m. and the radio in my office is blaring, but I hardly register the sound. My thoughts are louder. I stand by the window, fingers grazing the cold glass, watching the people strolling through downtown Macon. They move so effortlessly, unaware that my world is about to shift beneath my feet. How can they be so oblivious to this moment? So blissfully ignorant of the weight pressing against my chest?

Across the street, a group of middle-aged men are gathered around a picnic table, their laughter rising into the air as they sip coffee, sharing jokes as though nothing else matters. The warmth of their morning feels worlds apart from the chill creeping into my office. From where I stand, the view is modest, but I can make out a couple walking their dog. They're wrapped up in conversation, too engrossed in each other to notice the dog's eager whining and frantic tail-wagging. I watch them, baffled by the simplicity of it all. How can they navigate their lives with such ease while I stand on the edge of what feels like the most pivotal moment of my career?

My hands clench at my sides as I lean against the window, the weight of the upcoming meeting pressing down on me. This is my world, right here, right now. As I watch from behind the glass, it hits me. Despite my turmoil, life outside goes on. The world doesn't stop spinning just because my heart is pounding. I'm jolted back to reality by a knock at the door.

"Come in," I say, taking a deep breath as I walk back to my desk.

"Hey, Ms. Parkens." My assistant Tanya peers through the door before slowly walking in. "I'm sorry to bother you, and I know today is a big day for you, but Mr. Chestly is here. He mentioned he doesn't have an appointment, but he was hoping you might be willing to see him."

I let out a heavy sigh. "Mr. Chestly," I say with subtle irritation. "Why am I not surprised? Go ahead, Tanya. Send him in."

James Chestly, CEO of Clear Communications Incorporated—CCI, as they're known. I bumped into him at a programming convention in Atlanta about two years ago. Once he realized I owned Hot 108, our conversation shifted from vague weather talk to specific compliments about my station's turnaround in the local market. He mentioned CCI's interest in expanding its reach by acquiring stations in markets where they had minimal presence. CCI's board members and their C-suite were eager to discuss potential collaborations, partnerships, and even mergers. I clarified that I had no intention of selling to a large media company, because we were thriving. At that time, we had increased our market share across all demographics, secured advertising revenue from major brands, and boasted the top-rated morning show in the area with talks of syndication. We were on top.

James has periodically kept in touch—A message here, a bouquet there, and the occasional dinner invitation to "talk business." I never accepted, but I can't deny the effort. He's a striking man, after all—well put together, always impeccably groomed. His suits look like they were made for him, with a fit that's too perfect to be anything off the rack. And the cologne he wears—subtle but unforgettable. The kind that lingers just long enough to make an impression. But for me, business is business. And no matter how smooth he is, my interests lie elsewhere.

"Knock, knock." James pushes the door open and walks in. "Ms. Parkens, you look as beautiful as ever. Thank you for seeing me without an appointment, but—"

"Mr. Chestly," I interrupt. "I know why you're here, and once again, you're wasting your time. Frankly, today is not the day for this cat-and-mouse game. I would appreciate it if you would leave."

"Ms. Parkens, I really wish you would call me James," he says, flashing a charming smile. "I understand why you might assume you know why I'm here today of all days, but it's not what you think."

"Oh . . . ?" I say, with a hint of intrigue in my voice.

"Yes, I'm here to extend an invitation to the opening of a new restaurant, belonging to one of CCI's new clients, in Atlanta this weekend. It's going to be a star-studded event, complete with a red carpet and photographers. The owner is making a big push to promote their fourth location and has enlisted CCI as the media sponsor. I would really like you to join me this weekend, and I'm not taking no for an answer."

I'm slightly shocked by his assumption that I would agree to accompany him. Over the years, his usual hints at asking me on dates always came disguised as an interest in a partnership between our respective companies, but he's never been this bold or assertive.

"Ms. Parkens," he says after a few moments of silence.

"Uh . . . Mr. Chestly."

"Please, call me James."

"Okay, James. I have a very important day ahead, and I need some time to check my schedule to see if I'm available this weekend," I say, knowing full well that I am. "Let me get back to you this afternoon."

"Well, I'll give you the benefit of the doubt since I did drop in unannounced. But please know that I'm a man of follow-up, and I'll be reaching out to you later this evening. You still have the same number, right?"

He flashes that charming, distracting smile.

"Yes, I do."

"Perfect. Well, have a productive day, and I'll speak with you later."

With that, I watch Mr. Chestly leave my office. The encounter strangely lingers in my mind. James Chestly showed up in my office, asking for my company and insisting that he wouldn't take no for an answer. It seems genuine, but after years of discussions about acquiring my station, I can't help but wonder if there's an ulterior motive—especially today, the day our ratings dived. It feels too coincidental. It takes a moment for me to collect myself and refocus on the upcoming meeting.

I'm about to meet with all the department heads to review our market rankings, and it won't be pretty. For the third consecutive quarter, we've dropped in our key demographic—females aged 25 and up—and fallen from the top station in the market to number eight. This decline translates into lost revenue, fewer brand deals, and reduced advertising. I've been relying on my savings to keep us afloat, but that's beginning to run low.

Looking back on all the times Mr. Chestly has offered to acquire my station, I'm now considering whether it's worth entertaining. We've been the number one station in the Macon market for five years, so this unexpected and persistent decline is unsettling.

The competition is stiff, with only a few radio stations in the market—country, rock, and oldies—but just two Black-owned stations . . . 87.9 FM and mine, Hot 108. Sometimes, I wonder if I should have listened to my mother and become a nurse, as she always suggested. I can almost see my name badge: Angela Parkens, BSN, RN. But then, I smile and remind myself that I chose my path. A mistake my mom harps on each time we speak, every six months. "By now you would own the hospital, Angela," she would continue. "And your name would not be on a badge but the side of the building."

Just for this meeting, however, I may need to channel my mom's attitude in order to get through this day. I'm wondering how she would handle this upcoming meeting. No doubt she would be fearless, assertive and to the point. 'Command the room, Ann' I can hear her say. 'Never let the enemy know they have you by the balls.'

She always had a way with words. Whatever thought popped in her head, it came out of her mouth. No foul language, but the way she formed her sentences could cut through the toughest leather. If the truth made people uncomfortable, so be it. She wasn't in the business of comfort.

Delores Parker. A name that commanded respect whenever it was spoken and in whomever it was spoken to. She owned any room she stepped into. At sixty-four years old, Dee, as I was instructed as a child to call her, made people straighten their backs and measure their words. Her skin, a rich and deep mahogany, gleamed against her tailored suits, always in bold colors—deep crimson, royal blue, emerald green. Nothing about her was soft or uncertain.

Dee built Parker Strategies, a corporate consulting firm, from the ground up in the late 80s when black women in boardrooms were rare. She outmaneuvered men who underestimated her, outworked rivals who doubted her, and out talked anyone who tried to silence her.

I am her only child, and growing up in the shadow of such an intelligent and powerful woman was always intimidating. Being mostly cared for by my grandmother, I assumed Dee felt like all the missed dinners and recitals were necessary so I would never have to fight the same battles she had to fight.

Dee never mentioned the man that fathered me, and I never wanted to disrespect her work-hustle mindset to ask about him. I would drop hints to my grandmother from time to time to see if she would give me a name, but each time, I would always get a side-eye look followed by, "Chile, that's a story for another time." That time never came. So I just stopped asking. Now that I'm an adult, I don't feel the need to know anymore because I have bigger goals to accomplish, although I sometimes wonder if my relationships with men would be different if I had a father in my life.

Dee certainly had goals set for my life, and wondering if I live up to those goals often eats away at me, because here I am fighting to maintain something men have been trying to take from me for years. Although I am nothing like my mother when it comes to the treatment of others, my business acumen is all Dee. I refuse to be defeated.

In this business, you have to be cautious. I've learned that sharks come in all forms, and people you think are your friends can turn on you for their benefit. That's why I need to make sure James Chestly doesn't fall into that category. I need to protect my station—and my heart.

Owning my station and being a woman in a male-dominated industry has taught me countless lessons about whom to trust and, more importantly, whom not to trust. I think about the struggles I've faced—jealousy, betrayal, and heartache—and I question if it's all been worth it. Sometimes, I'm not sure. But for now, I need to focus on the meeting ahead and figure out how to address our slipping ratings.

As I'm lost in thought, the sound of my phone ringing pulls me back to the present. Seeing that it's my friend Brianna, I answer.

"Hey, girl."

"Hey," she says, her voice full of cheer. "Before you say anything, I know you've got a lot going on today, but I just wanted to let you know we're all meeting for drinks at seven. No objections. We all need this."

Brianna's been my girl for over fifteen years. We met in college during our first year after taking a summer sociology course together. We ended up in the same study group and hit it off. It's funny because we both come from the same hometown, with several mutual friends, but we didn't meet until college.

"Sure, I'll see you guys later. And you're right—I'm definitely due for a drink."

Brianna and I exchange a few more pleasantries and then end the conversation. After checking my phone for the time, I sink back into my chair and stare at my laptop, hoping the numbers on the screen will change. Of course, they don't. The familiar frustration settles in. Just then, a song starts playing from my computer, the opening chords filling the room like a rush of nostalgia. My hand instinctively reaches to stop the player, but then I hesitate. Instead, I lean back, allowing the lyrics to wash over me. The melody is soft and familiar, and as I listen, something stirs inside me. It's strange how a song can transport you—pulling you back into a time and place you didn't even realize you missed. This song does that. It took me to a different world before I owned this station and before my life became consumed with market shares and business deals. It was a time when I saw things with fresh eyes, when success hadn't yet hardened my view. It takes me back to him. Him. For a brief moment, I wish I could rewind. Go back to that time when everything was different, when my perspective on life and love hadn't yet been shaped by all that has happened since. If only I could return to that version of me. But I can't. Not really.

A knock on my office door breaks the spell. Tanya peeks her head in, grounding me back in the present.

"The staff is waiting in the conference room," she says gently, her voice pulling me back to reality. I exhale, and the moment slips away as I refocus.

CHAPTER 2

ECHOES IN THE CORRIDOR

I rise from my desk, only to be interrupted by my cell phone ringing. I glance at the screen and see Craig's name. We've been dating for about five months. We met on a dating app, and he seemed like a good prospect. Even though I'm starting to develop feelings for him, I remain uncertain whether the relationship is worth the potential complications. I should have mentioned to James Chestly that I'm seeing someone, but Craig and I are still in the early stages, not exclusive. Besides, he has a habit of getting frustrated when I delay responding to his calls or texts. I answer the phone.

"Hey, C," I say. "I can't chat right now. I'm about to head into an important meeting."

"Uh . . . okay," he mutters, sounding skeptical. "Interesting . . ."

It's one of his favorite words when he's doubtful.

"Craig, please. Not now. I need to focus on this, and I'm already late."

"Alright, I'll catch up with you later," he says, hanging up.

I can tell from his tone that he's not pleased, but I can't address that right now. My business is struggling, and I might need to make budget cuts to meet our financial goals. I need to get through this meeting and possibly inform some staff members that they might lose their jobs or that we could merge with CCI. Craig will have to wait.

I finally walk into the conference room and take my seat.

The meeting starts with the operations director and regional sales director reviewing last quarter's figures, detailing the severe decline in our key demographic area. This marks the third consecutive quarter of losses, they point out. Shortly after going over all the charts and data they've collected, they leave the tough news to me.

"As part of the management team," I begin, "we've decided that the only way to keep the station afloat is to eliminate some of our 'unnecessary' day parts—or, essentially, some on-air talent."

This decision was made via email after the operations director saw Mr. Chestly leaving my office. He had known Mr. Chestly had made several merger attempts with CCI and figured this would be a good way for me to keep my station intact. I agreed. It pains me to know I'm about to tell some of my staff that they'll be losing their jobs. I try to soften the blow with a decent severance package, but it's a small consolation for those who have families to support.

The meeting drags on, even though I wish it would wrap up quickly to end the awkwardness. Finally, it ends in a somber mood.

I'm quick on my feet, heading back to my office, when I hear a familiar voice behind me. Tanya pulls me toward the control room.

"Hey, I think that was necessary for the company," she says. "Look, I know I can offer all the advice I want because I still have my job, but don't beat yourself up for having to do that."

"Thanks, Tanya, but is this supposed to be a pep talk?" I ask, my shoulders sinking. "If it is, it's not working. I hate it."

"Ann, you had to make a difficult choice, and I think you did what was best. But enough about that." Tanya leans against the wall and drops her tone in the way she always does when she's about to pry into my personal life. "What's going on with you and Craig? You never finished telling me about the date you two had last night."

With everything going on at work, I'd forgotten about the argument Craig and I had the night before, which is probably why he was calling me today—to check my temperature. He had invited me over for a movie. He made dinner—salmon, mushroom risotto, and salad. We enjoyed the meal, laughed, and he even served my favorite dessert, tiramisu. But when we moved to the living room to watch a movie, he spent most of his time scrolling on his phone and getting up every five minutes to "go to the bathroom." Fed up, I asked if I was interrupting something or if he needed me to leave so he could handle whatever was on his phone. I implied it must be more important than our time together. He seemed annoyed, and an argument ensued. He called me insecure and claimed he was texting his kids. I left. As I spilled my guts to Tanya, I noticed the look of distaste on her face at the story.

"What's with that face?" I ask.

"I don't know how you deal with these disrespectful men. The dating scene is in chaos; I know it's tough out there, especially for women like you. Successful, well-spoken, and business-minded."

"Yeah, I guess you're right."

"Are you planning to keep seeing him? He sounds like he could be a handful."

"Right now, I'm not sure. Maybe he was texting his kids, but honestly, I can't think about that now. I need to meet with human resources to sort out everything for the staff we just had to let go."

"Okay, but Ann . . . I mean, Ms. Parkens, you know I'm here if you need to talk, okay?"

I thank Tanya for being such a supportive friend—I genuinely appreciate her willingness to listen to my tangled relationship troubles. With a final, comforting squeeze of her shoulder, I turn and make my way toward the human resources office. The hallway stretches before me, my shadow dancing on the walls. Each step seems to echo louder than the last, the distant murmur of office conversations blending into a dull hum. The air feels heavy, as though it's thickened around me, creating a cocoon that wraps me in a slow-motion haze.

As I approach the door to HR, the world around me starts to blur, and time seems to elongate. The once-familiar office corridor morphs into a tunnel of shifting colors and muffled sounds. My mind begins to drift, irresistibly pulled back into the past. The memories start to surface, not with a sudden rush, but with a gentle insistence. I see flashes of long-buried moments—an old photograph on a nightstand, the aroma of fresh coffee mingling with a hint of perfume. The warmth of a different time brushes against me as if trying to ease through the veil of the present. I see the faces of people I thought I had left behind, their laughter and voices fading in and out like an old, half-forgotten song.

The room is impeccably organized, with neatly stacked files and a polished desk waiting. I step inside, and the door clicks shut behind me, sealing off the corridor's noise. The conversation flows past me in that room, and when I finally rise from the chair, it feels like I'm moving through thick fog. I push open the door to the HR office and step into the corridor, but everything remains a blur. Faces and voices are distant, their details obscured by the haze that clouds my vision.

I wander down the hallway, my steps automatic, my mind still lost in the tumult of the past. I reach my office, but the events of the journey are hazy and fragmented as if I've drifted through a dream. My fingers tighten around the handle of my office door, and as I slowly push it open, the everyday scent of the office hits me. The familiar setting of my workspace—a mahogany desk, impeccably organized files, and the quiet hum of the city outside—feels both comforting and alien. I walk toward the chair in front of my desk, each movement feeling detached as if I'm moving through a dream.

The transition is almost imperceptible; one moment, I'm in the present, and the next, I'm enveloped in a cascade of memories. They flood in with a relentless tide, vivid and visceral. Faces blur into one another, conversations overlap, and the intensity of emotions I once felt returns in full force. The room seems to spin slightly as I sit down, the sleek, cool surface of the chair grounding me in the moment. I am lost, suspended between the present and the past, each pulse resonating with the echoes of what once was. The memories, relentless and unbidden, weave their way into my consciousness until I am adrift in their embrace, disconnected from the reality around me.

CHAPTER 3

THE QUIET STORM

The year was 1992, my junior year at Milledgeville State University, and I found myself drifting in and out of focus during my Ethics in Broadcasting class. The professor's voice was little more than a distant hum as I gazed out the window, my mind wandering far beyond the confines of the classroom. Daydreaming had become my refuge lately, a way to block out the noise of my life.

I couldn't help but wonder if this class was even necessary. I considered myself an ethical person—so why was I stuck with a B+? It gnawed at me, especially since this was the only class I had for the spring quarter. I should've been acing it. But Kevin—Kevin, with all his drama—consumed my thoughts, affecting everything around me.

Kevin, my boyfriend of nearly a year, had been a constant presence in my life. But the relationship felt as though it had aged us both decades, worn down by tension and unresolved issues. His ex, Alicia, lingered like a dark cloud, even when she wasn't physically present. I had lost count of how many times we'd clashed, the jealousy and suspicion gnawing at me. I kept telling myself that she was in the past. Four years together in high school should have been ancient history, right? Yet, doubts crept in at the most unexpected moments.

Alicia had cheated on him—that much I knew for sure. It wasn't just a rumor; Kevin had told me, and I'd witnessed it firsthand. I was roommates with the girlfriend of his fraternity's president, and we spent far too much time at the frat house. I'd seen Kevin and Alicia together back when things were good between them. They had looked like the perfect couple, and it was obvious how much he adored her. His face would light up every time he spoke of her, his words dripping with admiration. He'd even mentioned once that he was thinking of proposing to her. I remember wondering what it must feel like to be loved like that—cherished so deeply by someone.

Then came that fateful day last quarter.

I was on my way to grab lunch when I spotted Kevin outside the student center. He was trying to play it cool, but something was off—his shoulders were slumped, and his smile didn't quite reach his eyes. I asked him what was wrong. After a brief pause, he told me the truth. He'd caught Alicia in bed with his roommate. My heart broke for him as I watched his face fall, hearing him recount the moment that had destroyed everything he thought he had.

From that point on, Kevin and I grew closer—much closer. He told Alicia it was over and that he wanted to be with me. They hadn't been together for months—or at least that's what he assured me. But in quiet moments, doubt would creep in. Was she truly out of the picture? Or was I just a temporary distraction from the heartbreak Alicia had left behind?

"Ms. Parkens, are you with us today?" Dr. Hicks's voice sliced through my reverie.

I had completely forgotten I was still in class. I loathed this course, but it was a graduation requirement, and Dr. Hicks was the only professor who taught it.

"I'm sorry, Dr. Hicks. Could you repeat the question?" I asked, feigning interest.

"I was asking about the invasion of privacy module," she said, her brow furrowing. "If an evangelist who preaches against illicit sex is found to be having sexual affairs, can he claim that this information is private and should not be disclosed to the public? Is it an invasion of privacy if it's reported in the media?"

"Well, Dr. Hicks, my perspective is that the media has an ethical obligation to inform the public if there's a societal threat. The First Amendment supports freedom of the press, and generally, courts uphold the media's right to report on privacy issues," I replied, tossing in some information from the reading assignment. It felt like a pile of nonsense, but at least I was coherent.

"Thank you, Ms. Parkens. It's good to know someone did their reading," Dr. Hicks said, continuing her lecture. The class ended thirty minutes later and I was more than ready to be out of this room. I was supposed to meet Kevin at the café for lunch around 12:30 and according to my watch, I had about 20 minutes to spare. My stomach had started to growl during class so I was certainly ready to sit down and enjoy my meal. The cafe was about a fifteen-minute walk from the communications building so I didn't need to rush to be on time to meet Kevin. He was a stickler about being prompt and on time. I packed my books into my tote bag and headed out.

As I left the classroom, I spotted Sam sitting in the hallway. He was new to campus, and there was a rumor he was dating Alicia. I wasn't one to spread gossip, but I had seen them together often enough to believe it.

"Hey, Sam," I greeted as I approached him. "What's up? I didn't know you had a class in this building."

"What's up, Ann?" he said, giving me a friendly hug. "Yeah, you know life is different here at MSU. I switched my major last quarter to public relations, so I'm heading to a PR class. By the way, I was listening to the college radio station the other night. I heard your show. Dope! You sounded good, girl. 'The Bedroom Boom'—that's a trip. I can get into dem slow jams."

"Hey, thanks for tuning in," I chuckled. "I enjoy doing the radio thing. I took broadcast journalism last quarter, and they liked my show so much that they asked me to stay on. It's just two hours a night, but who knows who might be listening? I could get discovered."

"Yeah, you might be on to something," he said. "So, what else is new with you?"

I realized this was my chance to subtly probe about his relationship with Alicia without making it too obvious.

"Not much. How's campus life treating you?"

"It's going okay. I've even met someone new. She's pretty cool," he replied.

"Really?" I asked, feigning interest. "And who might that be?" I asked sarcastically.

"Man, stop playing. You've probably heard the rumors about me and Alicia. This campus is small as hell"

"Oh, right," I said, trying to sound surprised. "I heard something about you two. I hope things work out for you." I felt this was my chance. "But I have to ask—since you brought her up . . ."

"Sure, what's up?" Sam asked, leaning in.

"Well, when I was at Kevin's apartment last night, Alicia called around eleven p.m. Kevin told her he was busy, but she wouldn't leave him alone. It's becoming a problem. Kevin's asked her to stop, but she keeps calling at odd times."

"Really?" Sam asked, irritated. "She's been at my place a lot, but I work late shifts at the warehouse. I leave around ten at night."

"Well, she must be calling him as soon as you leave because it's getting annoying and that's usually around the time the phone starts ringing."

Sam's expression shifted instantly. It was rumored he had a bad temper, and seeing the look on his face, watching his eyes darken in just the few minutes we had been talking, made me believe there might be some truth to those rumors.

"Are you sure it's Alicia and not someone else calling him? I'm not trying to snitch on ol' boy but . . . you know," Sam suggested with a sly grin.

"I checked the caller ID," I said matter of factly.

I could see Sam continuing to get irritated by the thought of Alicia possibly calling Kevin from his apartment while he was at work. I think he wanted to believe they had something solid, but just like me, doubts were starting to creep into his mind. I wanted to gauge Sam's reaction because this would let me know the type of conversation I needed to have with Kevin about my thoughts of Alicia calling. At this point, I felt I had enough to go on as I glanced down at my watch. With that, I wrapped up the conversation, giving Sam a little advice about his PR class, since I took the same class last quarter from the same professor, before heading to the café.

Kevin was already seated at our usual table by the window, waiting.

"Hey, beautiful," he greeted with a kiss. He stood to pull out my chair.

"How was class?"

"Great," I lied, not wanting to discuss the dull lecture.

"Listen, the frat's throwing a party tonight, and I have to take money at the door. I'll give you the key to my place since I'll be late."

"That's fine," I said. "I have studying to do anyway."

"I also got tickets to Six Flags for the weekend. Want to go?" he asked.

"Sure," I replied.

Kevin knew I loved amusement parks, and we went to Six Flags whenever we could. I feel that was the kid in me wanting to come out and play and Kevin tried to do what he could to foster that feeling.

We had a pleasant lunch, chatting about various things. Kevin mentioned that his parents' thirtieth wedding anniversary celebration was coming up, and he wanted to make sure I was able to attend.

Once lunch was over, Kevin headed to his next class, and I made my way to the student center, hoping to find a spades game.

At the student center, I spotted Amanda, a career student who'd been at Milledgeville State for eight years. She was the sweetest person and the best spades partner. Walking towards her table, I glanced around, catching sight of Alicia's sorority sisters gathered nearby, their voices mingling with the laughter of Kevin's frat brothers setting up for the party. The familiar, laid-back chaos of campus life was in full swing. As I was heading over to Amanda, who was waving at me from across the room, I felt a sudden pull on my arm. Instinctively, I snatched away and turned—there was Alicia, her nails digging into my arm with surprising force.

Before I could react, my backpack slipped from my shoulder, the weight of my books and notes hitting the ground with a thud. Her grip tightened; her eyes locked onto mine with an intensity that made my stomach twist. The noise of the crowd around us faded into the background, leaving just the two of us locked in that uncomfortable moment.

"I need to talk to you. Now," she demanded, her voice sharp and accusing. "I know it was you. I know it was you!"

"What?" I responded, startled.

"You told Sam about me calling Kevin, didn't you?"

I wanted to deny it, but what was the point? Either way, I knew this confrontation was inevitable, I just hadn't expected Sam to bring it up to Alicia so soon. Besides, it wasn't a lie.

"Was it untrue?" I shot back, my frustration mounting. "Was it a lie though?"

"You had no business talking to Sam, you bitch!"

"But I did!" I spat. "I did it because it is my business, too." I struggled to steady my emotions, gripping tightly onto my temper. The entire student center fell silent.

"What the hell is wrong with you?" she sneered.

"Look, Alicia," I said, forcing my voice to remain even. "Whatever you have to say, I don't want to hear it. So please, get out of my face."

All eyes were on us. Everyone knew our history, and the tension between us was palpable. I had reached my breaking point with her interference. Turning to leave, I felt a sudden yank—she had grabbed my shirt, and the fabric ripped.

"What the hell!" I spun around, fists clenched. Without hesitation, I landed a solid punch to her cheek. Pain shot through my knuckles, but adrenaline drowned it out. I tried to slap her, but before I could do more damage, Kevin's frat brothers pulled me away. Alicia's sorority sisters rushed in, dragging her to the other side of the room. I struggled against the firm grip of Kevin's friends, my fury still blazing.

"Calm down, Ann. I'm sure campus safety is on their way," one of them warned.

I was shaking, barely processing his words as officers arrived. Rage clouded my mind. Then, suddenly, impulse took over. I broke free, charging at Alicia. Chairs toppled, decorations tore, and in an instant, I was on top of her, throwing punch after punch.

Campus safety wrestled me off, restraining me as I thrashed against their grip. Moments later, I was being escorted to the on-campus security office, my breath ragged, my pulse roaring in my ears. This was my first real encounter with the law.

After a tense round of questioning at the security office, I was released—thanks to the campus safety director, who happened to have connections with Kevin's frat. As I beelined through the parking lot heading to my car, the anger still simmering beneath my skin, I heard my name.

I turned to see Brianna running toward me, her face etched with concern.

Brianna and I had been friends ever since freshman year when we had a sociology class together during summer quarter. We realized we were both from Macon, GA and were astonished by the fact that we knew some of the same people but never actually met. Other than our mutual friendships with the same people back home, she and I also had another thing in common. Our dislike for Alicia. While my dislike (I felt) was justified because of Kevin, her dislike was different. Brianna told me she had encountered Alicia on freshman move-in day in the dorms a few months back, as they were moving in on the same floor. There was just something about Alicia that Brianna didn't like. That was the one thing that we bonded over as friends. She went on to tell me she wanted to move out of the dorms for the summer into an apartment but was having trouble finding something affordable. At that time, I had just moved into a two-bedroom house after my mom visited me and hated my dorm. My mom felt it was not up to the standards of where her child should be living and immediately found a house that was more to her liking. But because Brianna and I had a mutual dislike for the same bougie individual, I felt she would be the perfect roommate. When I asked her to come by and look at the house, she liked it and moved in a week later. We had been friends ever since.

"Are you okay? I heard about the fight. I'm so sorry," she said, reaching in for a hug.

"Yeah, girl, I'm fine," I muttered, trying to collect myself.

"You need to calm down," she said, her voice laced with worry. "I know Alicia gets under your skin, but don't let her get to you like that. You're about to graduate."

I took a deep breath, letting her words settle. "I just wanted to get her out of my face. I mean, the audacity she has to confront me about her mess. I don't know how it got so out of hand."

"She gets under my skin too," Brianna said, placing a hand on my shoulder. "But look, you are the one with Kevin, not her. Let her be miserable with Sam and keep it moving, Ann. You know Kevin loves you and you know I have your back too. Don't let her ruin what you are building with your man," she said trying to reassure me.

"You're right," I said, exhaling. "You know what Kevin and I have been going through. It's been crazy. Seems like one thing after another, plus I'm trying to make sure I have everything I need to graduate in a few months, get this internship, and you know my mom has been on my ass to come work at the consulting firm after graduation. Even though that's the last place I wanted to be."

"You mean, you haven't told your mom about you applying for the internship at the TV network?" Brianna asked with concern. She knows how my mom can be.

"No," I said reluctantly. "First of all, I haven't found the right time, and second, how can there ever be a right time when she is always traveling and never answers the phone? I have so much on me right now. I guess the thing with Alicia was just the tipping point. Anyway," I said, exhaling. "Wait a minute, damn, girl, how did you find out so fast?" My surprise was evident.

"Terrance called me," Brianna replied, smirking slightly. "He was at the student center and called me when he saw Alicia grab your arm."

Terrance was one of Brianna's casual flings, a basketball scholarship holder with a well-earned reputation for playing the field. It always baffled me why she entertained him, but I suspected it had something to do with how he satisfied her. He'd even been caught cruising around with another woman in Brianna's car, yet she had forgiven him and carried on as if nothing had happened.

"See? He's always up in my business," I said, shaking my head. "Listen, I need to get to Kevin's before he's out of class. I need to talk to him about everything before he hears about it from someone else."

"Alright, girl. I'll call you later. And don't go kicking anyone else's ass," she teased, laughing as she walked away.

I got into my car and drove straight to Kevin's apartment. I had planned on letting myself in with Kevin's key and taking a long, hot shower but just as I was about to step out of my car, Kevin came rushing outside, his pajama bottoms slipping down as he stormed toward me. His hair was tousled, and he looked half-asleep—clearly, he had crashed after learning his class after lunch was canceled. One glance at his face told me he already knew about the altercation with

Alicia. Someone had filled him in about the incident at the student center.

Kevin despised drama, especially the kind that could tarnish his carefully curated reputation as the "perfect guy on campus." And now, I was caught in the fallout and if the issue involved me, it also involved him. If he'd heard about it before I had a chance to explain, I knew he'd be livid.

"WHAT THE HELL ARE YOU DOING? HAVE YOU LOST YOUR MIND?" Kevin yelled, his frustration boiling over. "INSTEAD OF ACTING LIKE A DAMN FOOL, FIGHTING AND SHIT, YOU SHOULD BE HOME TAKING CARE OF YOUR MAN. I CAN'T BELIEVE YOU'RE STILL FIGHTING WITH THAT GIRL. I TOLD YOU IT WAS OVER BETWEEN US."

Before I could get a word in, he spun around and stormed back inside, slamming the door behind him.

I exhaled sharply and trudged up the stairs, bracing myself for what was coming. Once inside, I spent the next few hours trying to explain, pleading with him to see that the fight wasn't my fault. At first, he shut me down, unwilling to hear me out. But eventually, he relented.

Our arguments were never brief—they dragged on for hours, tension simmering between us. Yet, more often than not, they ended the same way: tangled in each other, our frustration melting into passion. In those moments, the world outside didn't exist. Just us.

Despite the tension with his ex, I tried to understand. They had a long history, and no matter how much pain she had caused him, their past still lingered. But to me, Kevin was everything. A good man. Hardworking. Balancing school while chasing his dreams of owning a barbershop or becoming a physical therapist.

He had lost both parents shortly before graduating high school so he didn't really have a support system, being an only child. He paid his way through college by being the resident barber on campus and working as an apprentice at a barbershop on the weekends. I admired that about him. He didn't cower in the face of adversity. He used that as fuel to keep him going to achieve his goal.

In the midst of that ambition, he seemed to feel as though he had something to prove. Coming from humble beginnings, he felt as though the entire world was against him. I resonated with that sentiment. Even though my upbringing was far from humble, having to prove to the world my worth was something I struggled with from having a highly successful, overachieving mother. Kevin had a few personality flaws, but who didn't? In my eyes, he was perfect.

"Baby, I'm sorry about what happened today," I murmured as we lay together, my head nestled on his chest in his cold apartment. The air conditioning hovered around 67 degrees, and the crisp new sheets I'd bought for him were rustling beneath us. "Alicia just gets under my skin."

"Ann, I told you—I left her behind after she slept with my roommate. I don't want someone like that anywhere near me or my future family," he said, hugging me tightly in his arms.

Kevin often talked about the future—marriage, children, the life we'd build together.

"And, baby," he continued. "You know I can't wait for the day I get to make you my wife. I love you, Angela," he said, his voice deep with sincerity.

"I love you too, baby," I whispered, curling into him.

"No, if you love me, don't love me too. Just *love me*," he corrected gently.

I smiled and adjusted. "I love *you*, baby."

Then, nestled in his arms, I drifted into sleep.

CHAPTER 4

COMMERCIAL BREAK

The year was 1993. Kevin and I had been sitting in the ER waiting room for over two hours; my stomach twisted in knots of nausea and anxiety. When we checked in, the nurse handed me a vomit bag after I explained that I hadn't been able to keep anything down. I had been vomiting all night and now felt light-headed, my body screaming for water that I couldn't bring myself to drink. Dehydration had hit me hard—I hadn't sipped since the morning before, and it felt as though my insides were being wrung dry. This sickness had lingered for days, and while I wasn't sure what was wrong, I knew I needed help. Kevin had insisted on bringing me here, and despite his panic, he stayed calm, gently patting my back as I threw up for the third time. His face betrayed his fear. He hated seeing me like this, but there was a strange comfort in knowing he was by my side, even if neither of us knew what was coming.

Finally, after what felt like an eternity, a stout woman in scrubs appeared behind the glass, calling my name. Kevin helped me stand as we approached the window, where she pointed to a door beside her. He opened it for me, and a petite, elderly nurse greeted us.

"Ms. Parkens?"

"Yes," I replied, managing a weak smile.

"Follow me," she instructed, leading us down a dimly lit hallway. We stopped at a scale where she took my weight and blood pressure, then asked for the date of my last period, jotting everything down on her clipboard. She handed me a small cup with a line drawn on the label for guidance and directed me to the bathroom. Kevin was told to wait in the exam room across the hall.

After handing the cup back to the nurse, I joined Kevin, who gave me a nervous but reassuring smile. We sat there, hoping it was something as simple as the stomach flu that had been making rounds on campus. Thirty minutes dragged by before a knock came at the door. A medium-built man in his fifties with dark hair and glasses entered, flipping through a folder.

"Hello, Ms. Parkens. I'm Dr. Pinish Patel."

"Hi, please call me Angela. This is Kevin, my boyfriend."

"Nice to meet you both." He nodded before glancing down at my chart. "We've run some tests, and, well, it looks like you're pregnant." His words hit me like a brick. Everything after that sounded like garbled noise. The doctor's words drifted towards me like muffled echoes through deep water, recognizable, but impossible to hold onto.

Kevin, on the other hand, sprang into action. "How accurate is the test? Could it be a false positive? Can we run it again?"

His voice was calm but desperate, grasping for any possibility that would undo what the doctor had just said. But regardless of the answers, one reality loomed—at nineteen, I was facing the possibility of having a child. And my mother … God, she was going to kill me. This was certainly not part of her plan for me and my life. Not only did I not want to intern at her company, I now had to somehow tell her that I was about to have a baby. Unwed and pregnant. Two things that she despised. But then I looked at Kevin and my anxiety subsided. I wasn't alone. He was here. He would be with me through this—at least, that's what I told myself.

Somewhere in the back of my mind, I had suspected pregnancy but brushed it off. After all, I was on birth control, though I wasn't always diligent about taking it every day. Still, I hadn't let that thought linger. Now, here it was, confirmed.

The doctor continued, offering advice on managing my nausea and handing me samples of prenatal vitamins.

"Any other questions?" he asked gently.

I glanced at Kevin, whose face had gone blank, his mind far from the room. I turned back to the doctor, needing some clarity.

"How far along am I?" I asked quietly.

"Based on your last period, you're about eight weeks," he replied.

"Wow," was all I could manage, the word slipping out as I struggled to process it all. Kevin said nothing. Dr. Patel continued, explaining resources for first-time mothers and suggesting we sign up for childbirth classes. He handed me his card and told me to call if I had any other questions. I nodded numbly, picking up brochures near the exam table as we left.

The drive home was steeped in silence, both of us lost in the depth of what we had just learned. My mind kept circling back to how we were going to break this to my mother. Kevin didn't have the pressure of telling his parents, so that was one less worry, but my mom would likely disown me. She'd never take this lightly. She paid for my tuition, my car, my insurance, my rent, and even gave me a monthly allowance. I could already imagine her anger. But maybe if Kevin and I faced her together and explained ourselves, she'd take it better.

Maybe we'd even talk about getting married. I didn't know what lay ahead, but I clung to the hope that we'd figure it out together. Finally, after miles of silence, I spoke.

"Kevin, I know we're young, still in school, and this was not part of the plan but we have each other." I placed my hand gently on his leg as he drove us home. "We can figure this out. It's going to be tough, but I believe we can make it work. We just need to talk to my mom, we'll find a way, and it'll be okay."

Kevin remained quiet, tense.

"Kevin?" I probed. No response. "Kevin?" I said again. "Kev ..."

He interrupted in a tense and low voice.

"It's not gonna be okay. I'm in deep shit. What the fuck ..."

I blinked in disbelief.

"Kevin, babe, I understand your reluctance because my mom can be a bit intimidating. But I believe we can go to her as a unit. If we sit down with her and make her understand that we know we've made a mistake but *we* are going to handle this together. *We* will just convince her that *we* are still going to accomplish all the things set before us. And look," I continued, "this may not be ideal for us as far as timing goes but *we* will get through this. I'm not the first nineteen-year-old who has ever gotten pregnant. Besides, we will eventually be getting married anyway, this just moves the timeline up a bit," I chuckled. "And you know what? Saying things out loud kind of takes the sting out of the situation. *We* will be fine."

At this point, I wasn't sure if I was saying all these things to get Kevin to say something or if I was trying to calm my nerves. On one hand, I was glad I had an explanation for all the vomiting I'd been doing and that it was nothing serious, but on the other hand it was serious. I was pregnant, I was nineteen, I was in college . . . but I had Kevin.

At the next stoplight, he finally turned and looked at me, his face heavy with guilt. A sinking feeling took hold in my gut.

"Kevin, can you please say something?" I asked, slowly, dreading the answer based on the look of terror on his face. Once again, he said nothing, the silence screaming louder than any words could. As the light turned green and he drove on, I looked out the window trying to wrap my head around the reason he was taking it so hard. While this *was* a difficult situation, Kevin made it seem as though it was life and death. What was really happening? Just as we were turning in to the parking lot of his apartment complex, it hit me. My blood ran cold, and before I could stop myself, the words escaped.

"She's pregnant too, isn't she?"

Kevin turned and looked at me. Tears began to run down my cheeks and the only thing I was able to do was let out a loud scream that ripped up from my throat.

"ANN," Kevin yelled.

The screaming continued, harsh and angry and hurt, beginning to crack.

"ANN," Kevin yelled again, this time trying to defeat my volume. "Listen to me," he said, calming down.

I put my hand up before he had a chance to explain. "Kevin, tell me that what I just said is not true. Tell me that I am not carrying your child at the same time your EX-girlfriend is carrying your child. Tell me that I am crazy for thinking such a thing because, like you've been telling me all this time, you're done with her. Tell me, Kevin. TELL ME!"

Tears continued to pour down my face and breathing became more and more difficult as crying filled my nose with thick mucus, making it difficult for air to pass in and out. I felt like I was going to pass out. I started sweating and hyperventilating.

"Ann, give me a second, okay?" Kevin said as he parked in front of his apartment. He shut off the engine and turned to look at me. "You don't look well. Let's get inside and I will explain everything to you."

"You mean you have an explanation for how you got your current girlfriend and your ex-girlfriend pregnant at the same time?" I said, trying to take a deep breath between every other word.

"Ann, let's go inside," Kevin said. He opened the door and walked around to my side of the car. He grabbed my arm and I attempted to get up from the seat. The light headedness I was feeling increased as I tried to stand. The blood rushed from my head, I began to feel weak and dizzy, and I started to see black. The next thing I remembered was opening my eyes and seeing Kevin sitting next to me on the floor with his head in his hands. I was lying on the couch in the living room. Slowly, I opened my eyes and my head felt like I had been hit by a ton of bricks.

Kevin looked over at me as he saw my eyes open. "Ann," he said with a worried tone and placed his hand on my head gently. "Oh my gosh, how do you feel? Are you okay? You fainted. Do you need some water?"

"Y … Yes. Water would be good, thanks," I said groggily and tried to sit up.

"Let me get you some water," Kevin said. "Don't try to sit up. Just lay back."

He went to the kitchen and filled a glass with water from the faucet, no ice, and came back to the living room. Before handing me the water, he helped guide me to a sitting position. As I slowly sipped the water, I felt the color coming back to my face and began to gather my thoughts about the reality of the conversation we were about to have.

"Ann, before I go into everything," Kevin said. "I want to make sure you're okay. I don't want anything to happen to you. Let me know you're physically okay."

I cleared my throat and continued to sip the water. "I'm fine, Kevin. I'm fine."

"Are you sure?"

I gave Kevin a look of disgust. I was wondering to myself if he showed Alicia this much attention when she was sick. Was he caring for her and taking her to the doctor when he found out she was pregnant? As a matter of fact, when did he find out she was pregnant? How long was he aware? If Kevin was being honest about his faithfulness, then he had to have known she was pregnant for some time—according to Dr. Patel, I was eight weeks, so she had to be a little further along. Nine weeks? Ten? Then it dawned on me what I was doing. I was sitting trying to calculate how many more weeks pregnant Kevin's ex-girlfriend was than me.

"Yes, Kevin. I am sure," I said clearing my throat again. "Can you get to the point please?"

He took a deep breath.

"About a month ago, Alicia called me and asked if I could take her to the doctor. She didn't have a way to get there because her car wouldn't start. I told her I didn't think it was a good idea for me to take her but she basically begged me because it was an important appointment and she had exhausted all possibilities of getting a ride from anyone else. So I finally agreed. When I showed up at her place, she told me to come in and sit down because she needed to finish getting dressed. She went into the bathroom and came back with a pregnancy test."

"Kevin, let me stop you right there, okay? I don't want to hear how you found out about the results of a pregnancy test. I am more interested in the fact that you were obviously still sleeping with her while telling me it was all about us. You were constantly making me feel crazy for suspecting anything."

Kevin dropped his head. "I'm sorry, Ann. I know I messed up. I'm so sorry."

"How do you know it's even yours? Isn't she messing around with that new guy Sam?"

"Yeah, well . . . she told me before that dude ever got to MSU?"

All I could do was stare at him. "How far along is she?" I finally asked.

"Thirteen weeks."

"WHAT? You mean you knew an entire month and said nothing to me? When were you going to tell me? In the car, I laid out an entire plan on how to sit with my mother to go over all this. How do you propose we tell her that not only am I pregnant but her future grandchild is going to have a sibling the same age and I'm not having twins."

Tears began to pour again but no sound came from my mouth. I looked over at Kevin and I saw his eyes beginning to water.

"Ann, I love you. I need you and I'm sorry. So sorry." He placed his head in my lap while kneeling in front of the sofa and began to sob. "Ann, I love you. I love you!"

Weeks passed, and the sickness didn't let up. I was in and out of the hospital with dehydration, and Kevin was always there. But we never talked about Alicia. I couldn't face the fact that the man I loved had gotten her pregnant at the same time as me. How could he do this? How could he betray me like that? I loved him—deeply, stupidly, desperately. I couldn't tell anyone, not my friends, not my family. I was too embarrassed. How could I explain that my boyfriend, the man I had invested so much in, had gotten his ex pregnant while I carried his child, too?

One evening, after another ER visit, Kevin decided we needed to talk again. He looked at me, his face tight with guilt.

"Look, baby," he said quietly. "I know this is a mess. I made a huge mistake, but I have a plan."

"A plan?" I shot back, my voice sharp. "What plan could fix this?"

He fumbled with his words.

"Alicia doesn't want to keep the baby. She's made an appointment at a clinic in Atlanta. You could . . . you could go too."

My heart froze. "You're asking me to have an abortion?" I whispered, barely believing what I was hearing.

"Angela, we can start over. If you do this for me, we can have a future together. It'll just be us, I promise."

I stared at him, trying to comprehend the man sitting before me. The man I thought I loved was asking me to erase our future before it even started. And for a moment, I considered it. Maybe it was the right thing. Maybe it would make everything easier. Maybe . . .

What did he mean, if I did this? Was I giving him an escape plan?

The next day, I called Alicia to get the number for the clinic where she had her appointment so that I could make mine. Luckily for Kevin, I was able to get an appointment on the same day as hers. Kevin drove us both to Atlanta. Time went on, and Kevin and I stayed together through college, got our degrees, and moved on with our lives. We never talked about the baby or the abortion again.

CHAPTER 5

THE NIGHT SHIFT

The year was 1995, and moving was always a pain. With Kevin out of town at a fraternity conference, I was left to do it all on my own. Thankfully, my new apartment in Macon had an elevator, so I didn't have to lug everything up any stairs. It was a cozy studio right in the heart of downtown—perfect, except it wasn't furnished yet, and my cash flow wasn't exactly flowing. No way was I hauling the cheap stuff from my college house into my new apartment. I was heading in a new direction with my life, and I wanted my apartment to reflect that. It felt like a fresh start: a new apartment, a new job, and a new chapter, leaving behind all the drama from college with Kevin, Alicia, and the memories of the abortion.

I had a plan for furniture. My mom had just redecorated her house, so I was going to raid her garage and pull together a decent setup for me and Kevin. Even though the lease was in my name and Kevin was still working in that small college town of Milledgeville, I knew he'd be over all the time. I wished he were here to help me move, but I understood how important his fraternity business was. I could've waited another week for help, but I had to move this weekend. I was starting my new job at KIBB Radio on Monday—part-time on-air announcer and full-time production assistant.

Kevin had his degree in physical therapy, but his real focus was opening his barbershop. He worked full-time as a correctional officer to save up for the shop and was still involved in his fraternity's community events. Ambitious as always, I planned to support him every step of the way.

Once everything was settled in the apartment, I was straightening up when the phone rang.

"Hello?"

"Ann, what are you doing, girl?" It was Brianna. "You got plans for tonight since Kevin's out of town?"

"No, not really. Just trying to unpack before Monday," I replied.

"Well, get your shit together! We're heading to the club. The dancers from Atlanta are coming down. Are you game?"

Brianna and some of our friends had a thing for hitting up clubs where Atlanta dancers made appearances. Her friend Manika had a biology class at Milledgeville State with one of the dancers, Night Heat, and they'd kept in touch ever since. One weekend, we ended up at our favorite late-night breakfast spot with all the dancers after a performance. That's where I met Pretty Boy, aka Cory. We hit it off right away, and since Kevin was getting under my skin because of some Alicia drama, I didn't resist when Cory made his move. We stayed in touch after that. Pretty Boy became my go-to whenever I was mad at Kevin.

"Is Pretty Boy dancing tonight?" I asked.

"Yep," Brianna replied, amusement laced in her voice.

"I'm there," I said, grinning.

That night, I met up with Brianna, Manika, and a few other girls at the club. The moment I spotted Cory, I knew the night was about to get interesting. He looked incredible.

As soon as the music changed, he locked eyes with me and strode over to our table. Without hesitation, he took my hand and pulled me up on stage. The beat shifted to a sultry, hypnotic rhythm, and before I knew it, I was upside down, his mouth buried in the seat of my pants.

The crowd went wild.

By the time I floated back to my seat, I was smiling like I owned the place.

"Damn, girl," Manika said. "He was all up in your shit."

Brianna was laughing so hard she nearly fell out of her chair.

"Girl, you've got him trained. He walked right over to you!" she teased.

We enjoyed the rest of the show, had a few more drinks, and eventually decided to take the party back to my place for an extended girls' night.

Just as we got settled, my phone rang. It was 3:33 a.m.

For a split second, I thought it might be Kevin. But when I checked the caller ID screen, it was Pretty Boy. And he wanted to come over.

"Yeah, we're here. Come through," I replied, still in shock.

The guys arrived, and soon, the room was filled with laughter and easy conversation. At some point, Night Heat led Manika into the other room, leaving me and Pretty Boy to focus on each other. He started rubbing my back, his lips brushing against my neck. Before I knew it, I was pinned against the wall, his rock-hard body grinding into mine.

"Y'all need to take that to the other room," Brianna called out, laughing.

So, we did.

An hour of incredible sex later, we passed out until sunrise.

At six a.m., a knock at the bedroom door woke us. Night Heat was telling Pretty Boy it was time to go. He gave me a quick kiss before slipping out, and I lay there for a moment, still caught between exhaustion and satisfaction.

When I finally made it to the living room, Manika and Brianna were getting ready to leave.

"I've got to get to work," Brianna said through a yawn. "I'll call you later, Ann."

After they left, I wandered into the kitchen to grab some juice when the doorbell rang. I figured Brianna had forgotten something.

But when I opened the door, Kevin was standing there.

6:21 a.m.

If he'd shown up just a few minutes earlier, he would've walked in on everything.

My stomach dropped, but I forced myself to stay calm.

Trying to mask the lingering scent of sex, I pulled my robe tighter around me.

"Hey, babe," he greeted, pressing a kiss to my cheek as he walked inside.

Without hesitation, he headed straight for the bathroom, turning on the shower.

I exhaled, still in shock, and then made my way to the kitchen to start his breakfast.

I felt dirty.

But I also felt satisfied.

And as I cracked the eggs, I silently thanked God I hadn't given him a key yet.

CHAPTER 6

SIGNAL INTERFERENCE

The year was 1999. My alarm went off at seven a.m. I'm not a morning person, so I hit the snooze button a few times before finally dragging myself out of bed. Kevin was still knocked out. I quietly got ready for work, kissed him on the forehead, and headed out the door.

When I got to the radio station, Rhonda was sitting at her desk, looking mad at the world, just like she always did. She'd started a few months back as the new receptionist. A few years older than me, she had a five-year-old son. She'd been married before, but she and her husband had separated. Before the divorce was finalized, her estranged husband was gunned down at a nightclub. Now, she was suing the nightclub for wrongful death, hoping for a big payout. Money was a sore subject for her because she never seemed to have any. She drove an old car that constantly needed to be jumped and often asked me for lunch money. I felt sorry for her sometimes.

Even though she wasn't someone I'd normally hang out with, Rhonda and I had hit it off. We talked a lot and for some reason, I felt comfortable sharing things with her about my relationship with Kevin. I shared some things, not everything. We eventually started hanging out. Over time, we became good friends.

Work at KIBB was going okay. I'd become a full-time on-air personality, still doing production work as well. I was wearing myself out and wasn't getting paid nearly enough for the effort. I was good at what I did, and after nearly three years, I knew I deserved a raise. On top of that, Kevin and I were on shaky ground, yet again. What I thought would be a fresh start for us hadn't turned out the way I imagined.

This particular day began like any other. I had just signed on the air when my program director, Kickin' Keith Farley, walked into the studio. Keith was an intimidating-looking guy, but he was cool and had taught me a lot. Looking back, I probably gave him more trouble than I should have. "Annie," Keith said.

"Yeah?" I replied.

"I forgot to leave you a memo, but there's a new group from Atlanta performing at the Cherry Tree Festival. They'll be here around noon for you to interview on-air, alright?"

"Okay. Do you have any background information on them?"

"Yeah, their manager is faxing over a bio. I'll bring it to you as soon as I get it."

Keith left. During a commercial break, I put the computer on auto-pilot and decided to see what Rhonda was up to at the front desk. Before the new computer system, we had to physically press play for commercials and use CD players manually; I loved the automation of everything now, letting me leave the room if I needed to. Computers really were the wave of the future. "Hey Rhonda, what's going on?" I walked up to her desk.

"Answering calls. People ask the dumbest shit," she replied with a sigh.

The phone rang before I could think of something smart to say.

"Thank you for calling KIBB; how may I help you?" Rhonda answered. She paused, listening, then turned to me. "Hey, Ann, it's Kevin," she said, putting the phone on hold.

"Okay, thanks. I'll take it back in the studio." I headed back to the control room to take the call.

"Hey, baby," I said. "What's up?"

"I need you to meet me at six-thirty tonight. We're meeting some of my frat brothers and their girlfriends for dinner."

"Okay, I should be leaving around five or so. I'll see you when I get home."

"Great. Don't work too hard," Kevin said. "Love you."

"I love you, baby." I hung up and got back to work.

Lunch came around quickly. I had just finished reading the bio Keith gave me on the group I was supposed to interview. The group arrived on time, and Keith brought them into the studio. They called themselves Divine, and they lived up to the name—Divine, all four of them. Throughout the interview, the lead singer, Brian, was particularly flirty, and I did my best to maintain my composure.

By the time it was over, I felt like it had been the most perilous interview ever. While I was walking them back to Keith's office, Brian grabbed my arm and pulled me aside.

"Thank you for the interview," he said. "I hope you can swing by the club tonight and check us out. And listen, if no one's told you today, you are very sexy. Why don't you give me your number?" Brian flashed a sexy half-smile.

I started to blush but managed to politely answer, "I'm flattered, but I've got a man."

Rhonda rounded the corner and interrupted us. "Brian," she said, "Keith's waiting for you in his office to talk about the concert." Then she walked off. I noticed a slight irritation in her voice, but I shrugged it off.

I finished my shift and was heading back to my office when Rhonda called out, "Ann, Kevin's on the phone for you."

"Thanks," I said, picking up the phone in the break room.

"I can't trust you for shit," Kevin's voice hit me as soon as I answered. "Why are you always flirting with people you interview on the radio?"

My mouth dropped and my eyes rolled. I thought to myself, *Here we go with this again.* Kevin listened to my show all the time and while I appreciated his feedback, I grew irritated by him always checking me on things I talked about with guests, particularly the male guests. He seemed jealous when he didn't have to be. Maybe it was his insecurity over the fact that we had been through a lot over the years, but I was really growing tired of his accusations. In my mind, none of this would be happening if he hadn't made me get the abortion. He made me do it.

"Kevin, what are you talking about? That's part of my job," I said.

"I heard your show. Flirting isn't part of your job. Let me guess, you're gonna blow me off tonight and go to the club with them instead?" I was stunned. How did he know? I'd only just mentioned to Rhonda that I had to go to the club tonight and asked her if she wanted to tag along. I hadn't even called Kevin to let him know yet.

"Baby, I was going to call you to invite you to the club, but yes, I have to be there. Keith mentioned it to me after you invited me to dinner. I was going to call you and talk—"

Kevin hung up on me.

I stood there in shock, wondering what had just happened. Before I could collect my thoughts on the phone call, Rhonda came into the break room, her eyes red from crying.

"What's wrong with you?" I asked.

"My car won't start, and I need to pick up my son from daycare. I hate to ask, but could I use your car? Maybe Kevin could pick you up later?"

I thought about it for a moment, then said, "Let me call Kevin and see if he can help. By the way, I cleaned out my closet last night, and I've got some clothes for you in my trunk." I often handed down clothes to Rhonda—she could use them. I picked up the phone and dialed Kevin's number. Surprisingly, he answered, and his tone was much calmer than before. I asked if he could take Rhonda to pick up her son, and he agreed. I figured he wouldn't mind since he hated going to the club anyway. Besides, the extent of what Rhonda needed regarding her car repairs was above my comprehension, and she was arranging to have her car towed to her house; maybe Kevin, being a wiz at fixing things, would be willing to help deal with her car's mechanical issues while I handled my work obligations. After I explained to him what was happening, thankfully he agreed. We hung up, and I felt a little relieved, hoping things were starting to cool down.

CHAPTER 7

SHATTERED ILLUSIONS

Several years had passed, and working at KIBB had its perks. I got into all the clubs for free, enjoyed complimentary drinks, and made plenty of connections. My career was moving smoothly, and I had settled into a good rhythm. I had been promoted from an on-air personality to a full-time production director, which I thought would give me more time with Kevin. With regular hours and fewer parties to attend, I imagined we'd have more time together. But Kevin seemed to have other plans. We fought constantly over trivial things, and we rarely spent any real time together. I caught him in lie after lie, and I was left bewildered by the state of our relationship, yet I was reluctant to let go. I loved him deeply and believed that all couples go through rough patches. I was convinced that time would fix everything.

Kevin continued working at the Youth Detention Center in Milledgeville. He worked six days straight and had three days off. During his time off, I often tried to do something special for him, hoping to make him forget about our constant bickering. Despite my efforts, we seemed to be drifting further apart. We had so many ways to keep in touch—cellphones, landlines, pagers, a full orchestra of communication tools—and yet all I seemed to get was radio silence. Our intimacy had vanished, conversations were rare, and sex had become nonexistent. I just wanted him to be happy.

It was about 7:30 a.m., and Kevin was on his off rotation, having stayed over the night before. We had planned to visit a new restaurant that evening, but he spent the night complaining about how tired he was and how badly he wanted to sleep all day. As I looked at him, I wondered if he was dreaming about me. I longed for the days when everything was drama-free. When he finally opened his eyes and glanced at me, he would normally kiss me on the forehead. But this time, he simply got up and walked into the restroom.

As he walked back toward the bed, I said, "You know, I was thinking. Maybe I should call in to work today so we can spend the day together, since you're off."

"Um . . . yeah . . . that would be nice, Ann," he replied, getting back into bed and turning over to go back to sleep.

I figured he was exhausted, but I was eager to spend the day with him. I rarely called in to work, but I thought it was worth it to focus on his needs and try to rekindle our relationship. I called Keith, telling him I had a slight fever and would be out that day. He agreed and said he'd see me the next day. I lay back down and soon drifted off to sleep. Thirty minutes later, the phone rang, waking me up. The caller hung up before I could answer. I dialed *69 to trace the call.

"Houston Day Care, may I help you?" I hung up the phone. I didn't have any children, and neither did Kevin, so I assumed it was just a wrong number. I hung up and snuggled back under Kevin's arm. He rolled over and wrapped his arms around me, offering a comforting embrace. We spent the rest of the day and night in bed.

The next morning, I knew I had a lot of work to catch up on, so I woke up early and headed to the station. When I arrived and walked into my office, I was greeted by stacks of commercial scripts and production orders that needed to be finished, all scheduled to air next week. I had to write, assign voice talent, and produce them. Plus, we had our weekly promotions meeting, which I dreaded. Our general manager rarely considered ideas from anyone other than himself.

Even though work was busy and productive, the day seemed to drag on. I was hoping to leave work early to get home and spend more time with Kevin since today was his last day off. Valentine's Day was this weekend, and I already knew he would be working, so I thought we could go out to dinner or catch a movie tonight instead. I wanted to talk with him about our plans, but oddly enough, I hadn't heard from him all day. When I tried to reach him, there was no answer at the house. I walked up to the front desk to check in with Rhonda, but apparently, her son had gotten sick, so she had to leave work to pick him up from daycare. Keith mentioned she probably wouldn't be back until tomorrow.

I continued to chomp away at the mounds of work sitting on my desk. When I finally looked down at my watch, it read 5:45 p.m. I started cleaning up my desk and packing up, ready to head home, when my office extension rang.

"This is Ann," I answered the phone.

"Yeah, I thought so. I figured you'd still be at work when I called your house and didn't get an answer," Brianna said. "Are you ready for the weekend? We've got plans, so if you're not ready, get ready."

"Girl, where are you trying to go?" I asked, still cleaning off my desk. "And you know I stay ready to go." I laughed.

"Forget this place; we're heading to Atlanta. I'll call Manika and tell her to pack a bag before she goes to work on Friday because as soon as she's off, we're on our way."

"Yeah, I need to get away," I said with a sigh. "I haven't been out in a while."

"You've been stuck to your man, and I didn't know if you had time to breathe. How are you and Kevin, anyway?" Brianna asked.

"Hmmm, I wish I knew," I replied.

"What's that supposed to mean?" Brianna asked, puzzled.

I sighed again. "Well, things haven't been great lately. We fight over the smallest things, there's no intimacy, and we barely see each other. He's always working at that damn juvenile center."

"Damn, girl, I didn't realize y'all were still having issues. I thought you were fine."

There was a brief pause.

"Let me ask you this, Ann—do you think he's seeing someone else?" Brianna asked.

The question hit me hard. I hadn't considered that possibility until Brianna mentioned it. I didn't think that could even be a possibility because in my mind, Kevin would never betray me again, especially after the huge betrayal in college. Even though Brianna was my best friend, I never told her about the pregnancy. She may have suspected because I was always sick but I never actually came out and told her. Of course the circumstances surrounding the pregnancy were not the best either. I felt if I had told her about being pregnant, I would have also had to tell her about Alicia being pregnant and then I would also have to admit to having an abortion. That was too much.

"You know what, I hadn't thought about it. I've been so caught up with work and trying to make Kevin happy that it never crossed my mind. Do you think that's what's going on?"

"I don't know, girl. You can't always tell with men these days. I don't want to plant crazy ideas in your head, but if he's not with you, he's got to be with someone."

"Shit, you might be right."

"Hey, do you think he knows about that night we went out to the club with Cory and the others?" Brianna asked.

"No, he couldn't possibly know what I did that night. You and Manika are the only ones who know, and I'm sure neither of you mentioned it to him."

"You know I haven't said anything! Look, Kevin seems like a good man who isn't the cheating type. Maybe there's another reason for his behavior. You've been working a lot, too, so it might be that. Besides, you've been together for several years. You just need to reconnect."

"Yeah, you're right. I just need to make sure he knows that I love him. Reconnect as you say. I don't want to start snooping through his things because I don't have that kind of energy. Besides, he knows if I found out he was cheating, I'd be furious."

We both laughed.

"Anyway, yeah, I'm all set for Valentine's Day. I don't want to spend it alone, so my bag will be packed and ready."

We hung up, and I was excited about spending Valentine's with the girls, even though I wished it could be with Kevin. Well, Cory would have to do since Kevin was working. I got up from my desk, walked towards the door, and heard a rustling sound. I opened the door to find Rhonda standing there, looking nervous.

"What are you doing?" I asked sternly. "I thought you left to go pick up your son?"

"Uh . . . I was on my way home and saw your car in the parking lot. I wanted to check to see if you were okay. I heard you on the phone, and I was about to knock when you opened the door. You startled me," she said, trying to laugh it off before patting me on the shoulder.

"Thanks," I said, "I'm good about to head home and spend some time with Kevin."

Her nervousness was odd, and I wondered why she seemed so unsettled. I wasn't really trying to think anymore about Rhonda, but I made it to my car and drove home. When I pulled up at my apartment, I saw Kevin's car in the parking lot. A smile came over my face as I hurried to my front door. Even though I hadn't been able to reach him most of the day, I still stopped by the grocery store to pick up food for his favorite meal: cubed steak and Caesar salad, accompanied by a nice glass of wine. By the time I got home, it was around 7:30 p.m., and Kevin was sitting on the couch watching television.

"Hey, babe," I said, walking through the front door. "I bought groceries to cook. Give me a second to get settled, and I'll have dinner started in a few."

"Yeah . . . okay," he said, unmoved.

I sat the groceries on the kitchen table and walked into the bedroom to change into something comfortable to cook in. I heard Kevin go into the bathroom as I threw on some form-fitting leggings and a T-shirt branded with the letters of the station where I worked. If this was going to be the night I had in mind for us, I knew that once I was done cooking, we would probably take a shower together and end up making love. I walked back to the kitchen and started taking the groceries out of the bag so I could get dinner started. I anticipated that Kevin would eventually come into the kitchen with his usual greeting of a kiss and hug and "How was your day?" After about twenty minutes, no Kevin. I peeked around the corner and saw the bathroom door was open. I then looked down the hall to see the bedroom door was now closed. I went over to see what was holding him up.

"Hey, babe, are you hungry?" I asked.

"Nope," he replied, irritation evident in his voice.

"I'm making your favorite—cubed steak," I said.

"I'm not hungry," he snapped back.

"What's wrong? Is something going on at work that you want to talk about?"

"Yeah, you could say that."

"How about a nice back rub?" I offered, hoping to ease the tension.

"No thanks. Don't you need to pack?"

"Pack? I'm not going anywhere," I said, confusion clouding my expression.

"Oh really? Aren't you and Brianna heading to Atlanta for Valentine's Day this weekend?"

I froze, my mind racing. How did he know I was going to Atlanta? I hadn't planned on hiding it; I just meant to tell him over dinner. He knew I sometimes went to Atlanta with Brianna. But how did he know I was spending the whole weekend there?

Kevin didn't like me hanging out with Brianna because she was single. He always thought her carefree ways might influence me. I had repeatedly told him that Brianna couldn't make me do anything I didn't want to do.

"Where's this attitude coming from?" I asked, my voice quieter now.

"I don't have an attitude. I just asked a question. Is it too much to ask for a straight answer? Forget it. You're always out with your girlfriends. If you want to be in the streets, fine, be in the streets."

"What are you talking about? I asked you to spend Valentine's Day with me, but as usual, you have to work," I said.

"Yes, I have to work! You don't complain when the money comes in, do you?" He turned and started walking toward the door.

"Where are you going?"

"Fine," Kevin said, turning back. "I am hungry. Let me change out of these clothes, and I'll come to the kitchen to eat."

We didn't speak again the rest of the night. Once Kevin sat down at the dinner table, the silence stretched into a gulf between us. I knew it would be a restless night. Despite everything, Kevin mumbled a goodnight before heading to bed. I replied, went into the bathroom for my nightly routine, and climbed into bed, turning my back to him. It was eleven p.m.

I tossed and turned, replaying Kevin's words. I wanted to enjoy my weekend away, but the argument had soured my mood. I felt stuck between a rock and a hard place—juggling work, my personal life, and our increasingly troubled relationship. I tried to focus on my breathing, but my mind wouldn't quiet. I couldn't sleep.

I dozed off briefly, only to wake up a few hours later. The clock on my nightstand blinked at 2:30 a.m. I stared at the wall on my side of the bed, not wanting to move too much and risk waking Kevin, who was a light sleeper. I didn't want to spark another heated conversation like before dinner. As I lay there, I thought about how unpredictable Kevin's moods had become. How long could we keep going like this? We had already been through so much together, and I didn't want to rock the boat, but I feared losing him.

I slowly turned over to look at him. Reaching out, I brushed my hand across the pillow where his head should have been. But it wasn't him. I sat up in bed, realizing Kevin wasn't there. I reached for the nightstand and turned on the light. No Kevin. My heart began to race, a sharp thud in my chest.

I walked to the bathroom and knocked on the door. No response. I checked the living room, thinking maybe he was sprawled on the couch, watching television. No Kevin. My pulse quickened as I moved into the kitchen—still nothing.

I stood in the middle of my eight-hundred-square-foot apartment, my mind racing. Where the hell could he be at this hour? I walked back to my room, threw on some sweatpants and a sweatshirt, and headed downstairs to the parking lot. His car was gone.

Back in the apartment, I sat at the dining table, replaying everything in my head, trying to piece together where he could have gone. Before I knew it, two hours had passed. The sound of keys rattling at the door snapped me out of my thoughts. Slowly, it creaked open.

Kevin.

"Where the hell have you been?"

He barely glanced at me as he stepped inside. "What are you doing up? It's four in the morning."

"I KNOW WHAT TIME IT IS!" I screamed, my voice shaking with anger.

"Oh … I couldn't sleep, so I went to the grocery store and browsed through some magazines." He shrugged, his tone eerily nonchalant. "You know I want to buy a house, so I was looking at magazines for construction ideas."

He spoke as if I hadn't just yelled at him—as if I wasn't seething, as if the explanation he gave was normal and I was the one out of pocket.

"You must think I'm a fool. Who is she? What's the bitch's name?"

Kevin scoffed. "Ann, you're crazy." He shut the door behind him and walked inside, calm in a way that made my stomach turn.

"I'm doing this for us," he continued. "I want our house to be perfect. Look, the conversation we had earlier got out of hand. You need time for yourself—spend it with your girls. I was wrong to question you. Baby, I love you so much."

He pulled me into his arms and kissed me, his tongue forcing its way into my mouth. It was like a slow, lingering breath. Safe, familiar, and comforting. It was as if the world faded away.

For a split second, I let myself melt into him. And then it hit me—the smell.

I knew that scent.

I jerked back, staring at him, my breath caught in my throat. It was so familiar, too familiar. The realization sat just at the edge of my mind, teasing me, taunting me. Without another word, Kevin released me from his grip and disappeared into the bathroom.

The weekend had finally arrived, and I was ready for this getaway with Brianna and Manika. I needed a break—from Kevin, from the fights, from the nagging feeling in my gut that something wasn't right. But no matter how hard I tried to shake it, it clung to me.

I left the radio station around 6:45 p.m. on Friday and headed straight to Brianna's. It had been a productive day—Rhonda had called in sick again, so I wasn't bombarded by her constant interruptions. That woman had a knack for showing up at my office every five minutes with pointless chatter.

When I arrived at Brianna's apartment, Manika was already there. They were perched in the kitchen, sipping amaretto sours. As soon as I walked in, they poured me a glass.

"Hey!" Manika grinned. "Is yo' ass ready to hit the road? We're about to get our party on. I called Troy, and guess who wants to see you?"

"Oh Lord, who?" I asked.

"Cory."

Brianna walked over to me, a playful smile on her face. "Mmm .. . and you know how he puts it down."

I was still upset about the Kevin incident from last night and couldn't shake it from my mind. Manika and Brianna noticed something was off because, even at the mention of Cory, I would normally light up or blush. This time, though ... I gave them nothing.

"Girl, what is wrong with you? I mentioned Cory's name, but you didn't even flinch. Are you ready for this or what?"

I sat at the table for a moment, my thoughts heavy. After a few minutes of silence, nearly on the verge of tears, I said, "I think Kevin is messing around with Rhonda."

"WHAT?" they both exclaimed in unison.

"Girl, NO," Brianna said. "That's your girl. She wouldn't do you like that!"

"Yeah," Manika chimed in. "Why would he go for her? I've seen Rhonda, and she seems like an unmotivated chick who's all about a free ride with no future. Didn't you say she's always hitting you up for money? Why would Kevin try to mess up your relationship with her? Even if you two are having problems."

"Yeah, I know this might sound crazy, but last night, Kevin and I got into a fight about me going to Atlanta," I started explaining.

"He didn't want you to go?" Manika asked.

"No, that's the crazy part," I said. "He brought it up before I had a chance to tell him. Then, after we went to bed, I woke up around 2:30 a.m., and Kevin was gone."

"Gone where?" Brianna asked.

"To look at magazines at the grocery store," I explained, rolling my eyes. "That was the lame excuse he gave me when he finally got back at four a.m. And what's worse, he smelled like Rhonda's musty-ass apartment and that cheap perfume—the kind she buys from that booster. You know, the one who comes to the station selling those purses."

Brianna and Manika laughed, trying to convince me that I was losing it and that what I was thinking couldn't possibly be true. But I just couldn't shake the feeling. I drank three more amaretto sours before I walked out the door behind Brianna and Manika, heading for Atlanta, hoping it would help me get my mind off Kevin and Rhonda.

CHAPTER 8

BETRAYAL IN THE AIR

Valentine's night was far from over. After leaving the club, Brianna, Manika, and I were starving, so we headed to our favorite late-night breakfast spot—the ultimate after-club indulgence. Or at least, that's what I thought. To our surprise, Cory and his crew were there too.

We slid into a booth behind them, catching up and laughing over plates of pancakes and bacon. The night felt surreal, as if we were all floating on the same wave of intoxication and camaraderie. After eating, we drove to Manika's mother's house, and a wave of sentimentality hit me. Maybe it was the crisp night air or the five tequila shots I had at the bar, but suddenly, I missed Kevin. Despite my anger at him for working on Valentine's Day, I wanted to hear his voice.

The whole Rhonda situation still gnawed at me, but I pushed it aside. I borrowed Brianna's new cell phone—my phone's battery was dead—and dialed the Youth Detention Center where Kevin worked.

It would've been easier if Kevin were allowed to bring his personal cell into work.

"Youth Detention Center, Ron 209," a familiar voice answered. It was Ron, one of Kevin's shift mates I'd met a few times at the detention center's family picnics.

"Hey Ron, this is Angela. Can I speak with Kevin?"

"Hey, Angela," Ron replied, a hint of confusion in his voice. "Umm . . . Kevin's not working tonight. He's off."

"What? He told me he switched shifts to get some overtime."

"Let me double-check the schedule, he may be working in another building." Papers shuffled in the background before Ron returned. "Nope, Kevin requested the night off two weeks ago."

"Okay, um, thanks, Ron," I said.

"You bet, Angela," Ron said and we hung up.

My heart sank and my mind began spinning. The ride to Manika's house for me was silent. Manika and Brianna had the music blasting and the windows down with the sound of the city surrounding us but I heard nothing but my heartbeat. The pain of a possible betrayal from my man and one of my good friends was becoming more and more evident. Years ago, Kevin promised me he would never betray me again. After I did him a favor, as he put it, and aborted our child so that his reputation wouldn't be tarnished by having two children by two different women, I knew he would not do this. I knew he would not sleep with one of my good friends. Not Kevin. Not another betrayal. Not again. But where was he, and why would he lie about working on Valentine's weekend? I tried to dismiss my worry, but the knot in my stomach only tightened.

We arrived to Manika's house and Brianna wanted to stay up and play a drinking game but all I wanted to do was shower and sleep.

"Ann," Brianna said with disappointment in her voice. "Girl, you can think about work on Monday but for now, let's have some more drinks and chill."

"Ya'll, I hate to be a spoiler but I'm really tired. I just want to go to bed."

"Ann, you know we are your girls," Manika said reassuringly. "If you have something you need to talk about, then let's talk about it. You don't have to pretend with us. We know you were worried about Kevin earlier and if there is something you need to get off your chest, let's hear it."

I smiled at them with appreciation on my face. It was nice to hear they were concerned about what I was going through but I really didn't want to hash out any of my feelings tonight. I had been drinking and if I started talking about my feelings, I would probably get mad, drive back to Macon, and start looking for Kevin. None of which needed to happen in the state of mind I was in. After they both realized I wasn't going to budge on having a conversation, Manika walked over and gave me a hug.

"Okay, Ann, we are here when you wanna talk. Meanwhile, the towels are in the hall closet and the soap is in the shower. Have a nice shower and if you want to talk when you get out, we are here. If not, I'm putting your blanket and pillow on the pull-out sofa so you can go to sleep.

"Thanks, girl," I said with tears beginning to well up in my eyes. I walked in the bathroom and turned on the faucet. I waited for the water to heat up before I stepped in. I inhaled the steam and began to have a silent cry. My knees buckled and I sat down in the tub and let the water run over me. I couldn't tell the difference between tears running down my face or the water from the shower but it felt good. I must have been in the bathroom for over an hour, not really taking a shower but enjoying the feeling of the water rushing over my body. I finally mustered up the strength to get out of the tub and dry off. I put on my pajamas and headed straight for the pull-out. Manika and Brianna were laughing and playing cards. When they saw me walking towards the couch, they both looked at me and smiled. I gave them an 'I'm okay' head nod, climbed onto the bed, pulled the covers over my head, and closed my eyes.

It was finally Monday morning and I had to get myself together and ready for work. I hadn't heard from Kevin all weekend and when I arrived home Sunday afternoon from Atlanta, there were no signs of him at my apartment. Where did he sleep? Thoughts of what he could've been doing all weekend consumed me all morning. The drive to work was filled with the thoughts of Kevin and Rhonda touching and kissing and . . .

BEEP. BEEP.

The guy behind me in a convertible laid in on his horn because I had apparently been sitting at the traffic light for too long. I wasn't sure how long though because, as usual, I was deep in my thoughts. I gave a polite, apologetic wave and made my way to the station. When I arrived at work, the first person I saw was Rhonda and she seemed overly cheerful, which annoyed me to the utmost, highest level of annoyance.

"Oh, hey, good morning, Ann," she said with a cheshire cat type of grin. "How was your weekend? Mine was woooonderful." She gleamed before I had a chance to answer. My annoyance flared as she prattled on about her weekend, oblivious to my tension. Why was she so damn happy? My frustration bubbled as she recounted her escapades, and when she started in on her sex life in explicit detail, I snapped.

"Rhonda, don't take this the wrong way, but you're pretty much a walking cliché. You don't have to suck every man's dick to keep one. And who knows what kind of germs you're picking up? Anyway, I've got work to do."

Her jaw dropped, but I turned and headed towards my office before she could respond.

Pieces were falling into place. Rhonda had always seemed too interested in my relationship with Kevin, and now, it all made sense. She was a backstabber, pretending to be a friend while sneaking around with my man. The weight of Kevin and Rhonda's betrayal pressed against my chest, suffocating me.

Before I could sit down behind my desk, Keith, the program director, stuck his head in my office.

"Knock, knock. Good morning, Ann," he said with a rapid tap of his knuckles on the open door before stepping inside.

"Hey Keith, good morning. What's up?" I tried to sound put together, but I was failing.

"I need you to fill in the mid-day shift for Toni Foxx today. She's out sick. Are we cool?"

"Yeah," I replied, my voice flat.

Months ago, I made the decision to focus on producing, writing, and voicing commercials and be more behind the scenes at the radio station instead of being on-air. It was a tough decision but I felt it was the best thing to do for my career and mostly peace of mind within my relationship with Kevin. He had trust issues with me having to be out at clubs each weekend as an on-air personality. As the production director, my hours were regular. Monday through Friday 9 a.m.–5 p.m., sometimes, depending on the load of commercials the sales team brought in.

Keith hired a new on-air personality, Toni Foxx, to do my old shift—mid-days from 10 a.m.–3 p.m. There were times, like today, when I would have to fill in for her for various reasons. Normally, I enjoyed being on-air, but today was different. Not only was my mind clouded with thoughts of Kevin and Rhonda, I also needed to focus on my own job. I had a stack of work on my desk that I needed to tackle, and furthermore, I had received a message a few weeks ago from corporate that I was up for an Addy. A local advertising award for the best commercials in the market. Apparently someone had submitted the commercial I wrote, voiced and produced for a local beeper company, and it had made it all the way through to the final round of voting. It wasn't my aspiration to win an Addy but it wouldn't hurt and would certainly look good on my resume if I ever decided to leave KIBB.

"Yo, Ann," Keith said. "You seem distracted. Are you sure you're good to fill in?"

"Yeah, Keith. I'm good. I just have to get some things in order here first but I'll be ready to be on-air at ten," I said, looking at the clock which read 9:15 a.m.

Forty-five minutes came and went and it was time for me to head to the control room to fill in for Toni Foxx. All the work that I thought I would put a dent in before I went on the air fell to the wayside as I stayed on the phone, trying to reach Kevin with no success. I paged him over and over with no call back, I called his mother and a few of his friends, but no luck. What was going on?

I was able to make it through two hours of the mid-day shift and it was now lunch time. At noon each day, DJ Razzle would come in and plug up his equipment to do the *Lunchbox Mix*. It was a live mix of old school songs which veered off our normal urban format during the rest of the day. The DJ came in around 11:30 to set up his equipment and get plugged in so his mixer would sync with the station computer. Whenever he came to the station, he would always stick his head in my office and say hello, or whenever I filled in for Toni, we would always talk about our favorite 80s music. Today I was a bit somber and not very conversational.

"Ann," DJ Razzle said as he started to hook up his mixer. "You aight? You seem out of it today."

"Yeah, Raz. I can't hide it. I have a lot on my mind. If you only knew," I chuckled and smiled.

"I feel you," he said, and with that, he started his mix.

As DJ Razzle mixed in the studio, I struggled to regain my composure. I had continued to try to reach Kevin for hours—with no luck. My thoughts wandered, circling the unsettling coincidences that felt too close for comfort. My mind refused to accept the possibility: my friend and my man. A double betrayal. Right under my nose.

Could two people be so calculating? I thought to myself. Would Kevin betray me like this—again? Especially after what happened with Alicia in college and the pregnancy? He wouldn't. He couldn't. Not Kevin. He loved me.

But doubt gnawed at me. I thought back to all the signs I ignored in college—how Kevin's affair with Alicia had led to us both being pregnant. I should have left him then. I should have walked away. But I craved love. The love I had never truly received. The love of a man. The love I thought Kevin could give me—but he didn't. Maybe that's why *I* started being unfaithful.

But with Cory, it was different, I reasoned to myself. To Kevin, he was a stranger. If they passed each other on the street, they wouldn't exchange a word. But this? This betrayal was personal. Rhonda wasn't a stranger. She was my friend. Someone I shared my thoughts with. My secrets. My laughter. And Kevin—Kevin was supposed to be my partner, my life. The weight of it was incomprehensible.

After hours of failed attempts to reach Kevin, something inside me snapped. Just try it. See what happens.

I picked up the phone one last time and slowly started to dial. I dialed Rhonda's home number from the studio phone but hung up before it rang. My anxiety surged, my breathing labored. I tried again.

I slowly picked up the phone and dialed the number again. This time, I didn't hang up.

The phone rang.

"Hello," a male voice said.

"Hello?" I said and instantly started to break out in a sweat.

My heart slammed against my ribs.

"WHAT THE FUCK ARE YOU DOING AT THAT BITCH'S HOUSE ANSWERING HER PHONE?" I screamed before slamming the receiver down.

The truth hit me like a lightning strike. The betrayal was no longer a suspicion—it was real. A gut-wrenching, undeniable reality. I was numb. My body moved on instinct as I fled the studio, my mind a whirlwind of rage and pain. I headed to my office to grab my purse and my keys.

When I stormed into the front office, Rhonda greeted me with her fake smile, her phone in hand, as if nothing had happened.

I lost it.

I lunged at her, knocking over her desk, grabbing her by the hair, and slamming her head against the file cabinet.

"YOU LYING BITCH! YOU'VE BEEN FUCKING KEVIN THIS WHOLE TIME! YOU WERE SUPPOSED TO BE MY FRIEND!"

Because of the loud commotion, the entire staff was now in the front office, witnessing my breakdown. The sales manager, the general manager, and a few sales executives, all watched me fall apart as I slapped and punched Rhonda. And once again, I was fighting a female over Kevin. At the moment, I didn't realize the irony of it all, because all I wanted was for Rhonda to physically feel the pain she had inflicted on me while smiling in my face and sleeping with my man behind my back for probably months.

Keith rushed forward, pulling me away, his voice drowned by the chaos.

Shaking, I snatched up my keys and purse and fled the station, my heart pounding so hard I could barely breathe.

I was devastated.

Kevin. Rhonda. My man. My friend. Their betrayal shredded me.

Tears blurred my vision as I climbed into my car, my hands trembling as I started the engine. The weight of my shattered world crushed me as I sped off, trying to outrun the pain.

CHAPTER 9

SHATTERED TRUST

I didn't know where I was going or what I planned to do. All I knew was that my mind was a whirlwind of thoughts. The fact that Kevin had been with Rhonda—touching her, holding her—and then dared to come home and tell me he loved me made me sick to my stomach.

I was driving recklessly, my hands gripping the steering wheel so tightly my knuckles turned white. Before I knew it, I had veered onto Interstate 75, heading south. My resolve was clear: I needed to get to Rhonda's house and confront Kevin—just as I had with that two-faced backstabber at the station. I might have lost my job, but these deceitful people needed to pay.

I arrived at Rhonda's apartment in what felt like mere minutes. As I pulled into the parking lot, my suspicions were confirmed— Kevin's car was there. He had backed into the space, a clear sign he frequented this place. He was settled in, comfortable, and not planning on leaving anytime soon.

Rage surged through me. I parked aggressively, my tires screeching as I nearly clipped his car and stormed toward her front door.

"OPEN THIS FUCKING DOOR, KEVIN! I KNOW YOU CAN HEAR ME BECAUSE I CAN HEAR YOU MOVING AROUND IN THERE!" I screamed, my voice raw and furious. I banged on the door.

Silence.

I pounded on the door again, harder this time. The tears had long since dried, replaced by a scorching heat burning inside me. Months of turmoil, doubt, and betrayal boiled over. Without thinking, I kicked the door.

It flew off its hinges, slamming to the floor.

Kevin appeared from around the corner, wearing a radio station T-shirt branded with the letters KIBB—probably borrowed from Rhonda—and the uniform pants from the detention center that I ironed for him every morning,

The sight of him standing there, so casual, as if he hadn't just destroyed my trust, sent a chilling calm through me.

"What the fuck are you doing here?" I muttered, my voice like steel. "I've been calling you repeatedly, and you ignored me—because you were with her."

Kevin's face twisted into something unreadable. "What are you doing here, Angela? Why are you freaking out? I needed help with my resume, and Rhonda was helping me."

I almost laughed. The nerve of him. Even caught red-handed, he was still lying.

My mind raced, replaying every unanswered call, every night he was "busy," every smug look Rhonda had given me at work. She had probably just rolled out of bed with him when she saw me in the office. The musty scent of her apartment clung to the air, and it disgusted me.

I couldn't hold back.

With a guttural grunt, I lunged at him, shoving him so hard he crashed into the laundry room door before hitting the floor, stunned.

I seized the moment, snatching his pager off the counter.

"LOOK! YOU HAVE SEVENTEEN PAGES FROM ME! AND YOU IGNORED EVERY SINGLE ONE!" I screamed, my hands shaking.

Before he could react, I hurled the pager against the wall. It shattered into pieces, plastic and glass scattering across the floor.

Kevin, now fully recovered, locked eyes with me.

For the first time, I saw something I had never seen in him before.

Rage.

Before I could react, he stood up and lunged in my direction. Once he got close enough to me, his hands shot out and wrapped around my neck.

He was choking me.

I gasped, clawing at his arms, my nails scraping his skin, kicking and thrashing with everything I had. My vision blurred, black spots creeping in at the edges. My body screamed for air.

Desperation fueled me. With one final surge of strength, I drove my knee into his groin.

Kevin let out a strangled grunt and released me, stumbling back.

Gasping for breath, I wasted no time. I swung with every ounce of power in me, my open palm connecting with his face.

Blood splattered.

My ring—my signet ring—had cut his cheek, leaving a jagged gash.

We crashed onto the floor, knocking over Rhonda's picture frames from the coffee table. We wrestled, rolling across the carpet, each trying to gain control. Time felt distorted—the fight seemed both endless and fleeting.

Then, suddenly—

"POLICE DEPARTMENT! DON'T MOVE!"

The sharp command cut through the chaos.

I blinked, my chest heaving, as two officers stood in the doorway, hands on their holsters. The front door was barely hanging on its frame, splintered from my earlier kick.

One officer's gaze swept over the wreckage—the shattered phone, the overturned furniture, Kevin's bleeding face—before his eyes landed on me and the obvious bruises on my neck.

"Which one of you lives here?" he asked, his tone firm.

I swallowed hard, my pulse roaring in my ears.

This night wasn't over. Not even close.

"Neither of us lives here, officer," I said, my voice trembling as I tried to regain my composure. My hands were still shaking, my breath ragged with anger. "This is supposed to be my man, and he was shacking up with my friend."

The officer turned to Kevin, his expression unreadable. "Is this true, sir? You don't live here either?"

Kevin hesitated. "No, sir, I don't."

"We received a noise complaint about a fight, and from the looks of it, they weren't wrong." The officer's gaze flicked from the broken door to the shattered phone on the floor.

Kevin opened his mouth, but the officer cut him off. "Ma'am, you have blood on your shirt. Are you hurt?"

I glanced down at my clothes, noticing for the first time the crimson splatters from where my ring had cut Kevin's face. "No," I whispered, my voice barely audible.

The officer turned back to Kevin. "Sir, do you live here?"

Kevin sighed. "No, I was just about to leave when she came over. A friend lives here."

"A friend," I repeated mockingly, my voice thick with bitterness. "I am no friend of that bitch. And neither are you." I shot Kevin a withering glare. "You were fucking her behind my back."

"Ma'am, I need you to calm down," the officer warned. "We need to hear the full story from both of you. Since neither of you lives here, you'll both need to leave once we confirm with the apartment owner that this isn't a break-in. I see the door is barely hanging on its hinges."

One officer led Kevin outside while the other motioned for me to follow him into the kitchen. He asked me about my relationship with Rhonda and Kevin, but I had no answers—just tears. I couldn't string together words that made sense.

Ten minutes passed, each second stretching into eternity.

Finally, the officers returned with Kevin in tow.

"I spoke with the apartment owner," one officer said. "She doesn't want to press charges. But as I mentioned, neither of you lives here, so you both need to leave. We'll remain on-site until you've driven out of the parking lot. The owner is on her way to assess the damage."

I nodded, swallowing back the lump in my throat. There was nothing left to say.

I stepped outside, my head pounding, my body sore from the emotional and physical toll of the night. The weight of everything crashed down on me as I reached my car. My hands trembled as I fumbled with my keys.

"Ann."

Kevin's voice cut through the air.

I turned around instinctively, even though I wanted nothing more than to disappear. He stood two parking spaces away, his face a mixture of desperation and regret.

"We need to talk," he said, his voice hoarse. "Can we meet at your place?"

My heart warred with my mind. I should have told him to go to hell. I should have walked away. But the word left my lips before I could stop it.

"Yes."

Tears still streaked my face as I slid into my car. In my rearview mirror, I saw Kevin get into his own and follow me.

The drive back to my apartment felt endless. My thoughts spiraled, replaying every moment with Kevin, dissecting every missed call, every unanswered text. Was he with her? Had he been lying to me this entire time?

And what now?

I loved him. God help me, I still loved him.

But love didn't erase betrayal.

By the time we pulled into my apartment complex, my emotions were a tangled mess. I got out of my car, wiping at my tear-streaked face as Kevin approached.

As we reached my front door, I hesitated for just a moment before unlocking it. The cool air inside hit my flushed skin, offering the briefest moment of relief. But the second I stepped inside, reality came crashing back.

"Ann," Kevin said, his voice shaking.

I turned to him, my eyes searching his face for an answer I knew I'd never find.

"What's happening?" I whispered. "Why were you at Rhonda's apartment?"

Kevin exhaled, running a hand over his face. "Why would you think I'd do something like this to you?" His voice cracked, his eyes pleading. "We've been through so much. You've always been by my side. I would never jeopardize that."

His hands found my arm. I wanted to pull away, but my body felt weak—too exhausted to fight.

He pulled me close, his touch surprisingly gentle. Soothing. Like he was touching me for the first time.

"Ann, look," he murmured, drawing me in. "I'm trying to leave the detention center. Rhonda offered to help with my resume, and because she works with computers, I thought she had the right software. This morning was the only time I could meet with her before she left for work. I ended up borrowing one of her T-shirts because I was tired."

His explanation sounded logical. Almost too logical.

My mind screamed at me not to believe him, but his arms felt like home. His voice was familiar, his touch intoxicating.

I didn't want to think anymore.

I stepped back, searching his face for any hint of deception, any flicker of the truth.

Kevin's eyes locked onto mine. Then, slowly, he leaned in.

The kiss started softly and hesitantly but quickly deepened. It was different this time—urgent, desperate, filled with something I couldn't name. I melted into him, my body betraying me.

Before I knew it, I unlocked the door to my apartment and we both stumbled inside, still in a deep embrace. Kevin picked me up and led me to the bedroom.

As his hands moved over my body, as our limbs tangled in the sheets, I surrendered to the moment. To the comfort. To the lie I wanted so badly to be true.

But even as we made love, a voice in the back of my mind whispered a painful truth:

This wasn't the end.

This was just the beginning.

Afterwards, lying next to Kevin, I stared at the ceiling, my mind spiraling with worry about my job. I had walked out during my air shift, likely damaging office equipment in the process. What excuse could I possibly give to explain my actions? No excuse came to mind.

The next morning, I walked into the radio station, trying to act as normal as possible despite the events of the previous day. Rhonda was absent from her desk. I assumed she had seen me coming and decided to avoid me. As I approached my office, I noticed an envelope taped to the door with my name on it: A. PARKENS. My heart sank, and I immediately feared it was my termination notice. I hesitated before opening it, only to find a memo requesting a meeting with Keith and the general manager, Mike Thompson, at noon. A small wave of relief washed over me—I still had a job, at least until then.

I spent the morning in my office, avoiding coworkers out of embarrassment and uncertainty about my future. At 11:50 a.m., I decided to head to the meeting early. My nerves were on edge as I walked to the general manager's office. When I arrived at the door,

I saw Keith and Mike laughing and sipping coffee. When they both looked up at me, the laughter halted. Keith gestured for me to come in. As I entered the office, I walked over to the side of the table where the two men were sitting and before I could reach an empty chair, Mike spoke up with a booming yet calm voice.

"Hello, Angela," Mike said sternly, his tone giving nothing away. "Please have a seat. I'm sure you know why we've asked you here."

I sat down, feeling the weight of the moment pressing down on me. Mike spoke about company policies and station rules, his words drifting into a blur as I tried to focus. Keith chimed in occasionally, but I couldn't fully grasp what they were saying as I tried to hold back tears that began to fill my eyes out of nowhere. When Mike finally asked if I had anything to add, I couldn't fight it any longer. Tears began streaming down my face. Keith handed me a box of tissues, and I struggled to regain my composure. I couldn't find the right words to explain what had led me to this point. All I could do was cry.

"Ms. Parkens," Mike said gently, his voice softening. "We understand you're going through some personal difficulties. We value your contributions to the station, so we're offering you a two-week unpaid suspension. After that, you'll return to your position. Do you understand?"

I nodded, my face buried in tissues, overwhelmed by the weight of everything. Keith patted my back reassuringly, telling me to clean up and head home. As I left the office, I couldn't help but wonder how I was going to fill the next two weeks.

CHAPTER 10

WHEN THE MUSIC FADES

It was Saturday night, and for the first time in months, I didn't have plans to go out, nor did I want any. Brianna had called me earlier that morning to let me know that she and Manika would be coming over around eight o'clock for our usual girls' powwow. I agreed because if I said no, I knew I wouldn't hear the end of it. Even though I wasn't in the mood to be around anyone, I figured a night in with the girls might be just what I needed.

With two weeks off from work, I wasn't sure what to do with myself. I didn't want to sit around and overthink the whole mess with Kevin and Rhonda. I still hadn't fully processed everything. Sure, we'd made love after leaving Rhonda's house that day, and Kevin had been nothing but a gentleman since, but something about the whole situation still didn't feel right. I couldn't quite shake the feeling.

I found out that Rhonda had quit her job at the station after our encounter and had seemingly disappeared. I overheard Keith and Mike talking about how difficult it would be to find a replacement receptionist on such short notice, but they both agreed Rhonda had

95

good reasons for leaving the way she did—whatever that meant. Still, I knew the girls were coming over, so I had to put on a fresh face and act like nothing was wrong, even though my mind was a whirlwind.

Eight o'clock came faster than I expected, and the doorbell rang while I was in the kitchen finishing up the nachos and dip.

"I'm coming!" I shouted, wiping my nacho cheese-covered hands on a dishcloth and rushing to open the door.

"What's up, ladies?" I said, forcing a smile.

"What's up, Ann?" Brianna replied.

"Hey, girl," Manika chimed in as they both walked inside.

"Dem nachos sho' smell good," Brianna said, setting her purse down on the couch.

"Oh, and we stopped by that wing place and got some lemon pepper wings, too," Manika added.

"Uh . . . where's the liquor?" I asked, trying to sound casual.

"Oh, yeah," Brianna said, as if she had just remembered. "I forgot to tell you. I know you and Kevin have been going through y'all's . . . stuff . . . so I figured you needed a break from all that drama. I invited a few of my friends over. Hope that's okay."

By now, Brianna and Manika were grinning from ear to ear, like they were in on some big secret.

"What friends?" I asked, raising an eyebrow. "And why don't I already know them? I mean, I know the same people y'all know. And where is the liquor?"

"Well . . . they're actually more my friends," Manika said, giving me an apologetic look. "I grew up with them in the A and they are bringing the liquor."

"Oh shit," I muttered under my breath.

Just then, the doorbell rang again, and I knew I was in for a wild night. Brianna skipped over to the door, but before opening it, she put her hand on the knob and took a deep breath.

"Okay, girls, are you ready for this?" With those words, she flung open the door, and in walked five of the finest men I had ever seen. Jermaine, Bryan, Robert, Patrick, and Ryan strolled in, each of them a jaw-dropper, and all I could manage to say was, "WOW."

Manika walked over to them, giving me the formal introductions. As I extended my hand for a handshake, each one of them gently grabbed it and pressed a soft kiss to it. Manika explained that they all worked for the same TV station in Atlanta and hit the same gym. They knew Manika from the gym, all except Jermaine, who had grown up with her. He was more like a big brother. After the hellos, I stood up to bring out the nachos and food.

"Do you need any help with that?" Jermaine asked as I walked out with a tray of wings and soda to chase the vodka we were drinking.

"Sure," I replied with a smile. He walked over, grabbed the tray of wings, and set it on the coffee table. I placed the soda next to the tray and was about to turn back to the kitchen when Jermaine gently grabbed my hand.

"Hey, where are you going?"

"I was headed back to the kitchen to get the rest of the food."

"I think we have enough right here. Why don't you come sit next to me so we can talk and get to know each other?"

I wanted to say yes, but I knew if I did, it would only lead to trouble. I was vulnerable because of everything with Kevin. I didn't want to believe he and Rhonda had been fooling around, especially after he looked me in the eye and denied it. He'd told me my accusations were outrageous, that I had to trust him, and that he'd never betray me—especially not with one of my friends. I wanted to believe him, but something about that day at Rhonda's apartment still didn't sit right with me. These thoughts swirled in my mind the second Jermaine asked me to sit with him.

"Uh . . . Ann," Brianna butted in as she passed by on her way to the kitchen, overhearing Jermaine's invitation. "Don't you think you're being rude? Jermaine just wants to talk."

Maybe she was right—it was just a conversation. I looked over at Manika and the others, laughing and playing spades, having a good time.

Sometimes I felt Manika and Brianna knew things that they weren't telling me. They'd never come out and told me I needed to stay away from Kevin but they'd never really supported the relationship. They had supported my feelings for him but never really told me I should fight for Kevin. Were they sparing my feelings because they'd seen him with Rhonda and they didn't want to tell me? It seemed, though, they were always trying to get me to do other things that didn't involve Kevin. Like spending time with other men. I sometimes didn't understand what that was about. I knew they were trying to take my mind off my troubles but all I wanted to do tonight was chill at home by myself. When Brianna mentioned they wanted to hang out, I said yes because I thought it would just be us, the girls. Now they had invited "their friends" and I wasn't sure if I was in the mood for all this.

"Hey, girl," Brianna said, giving me a little nudge with her elbow. "We've got this. Why don't y'all head out on the balcony for some privacy?"

"That's fine with me," Jermaine said, flashing a grin. "Unless Miss Ann thinks I'm gonna kidnap her."

I gave Brianna a look.

She smiled, nodded her head in the direction of my balcony, and mouthed the words, "*Go ahead.*"

"Uh . . . okay, sure. We can go out on the balcony and talk for a bit."

Jermaine smiled and took my hand. We walked toward my bedroom. How did he know where the balcony—or my room—was? I had the thought but didn't say anything. I followed him as if this were his apartment, and I was the guest. We reached the French doors that led to the balcony. I unlocked the latch, and Jermaine opened the door. We stepped outside and sat on the patio sofa. The night was cool, the air crisp. Trees and an artificial pond surrounded my apartment complex. From my balcony, you could see the tops of the trees and peer down into the pond. The night sky was alive with the sounds of nocturnal creatures, their song soothing to my ears. Sometimes, I'd leave the balcony door open when I couldn't sleep, letting the night's lullaby carry me to rest. Tonight was no different. It was a beautiful night, one I wished I could share with Kevin, but as usual, he was at work. Since the incident with Rhonda, he'd been trying to stay close, but I still had so many doubts.

"So, you're Ann," Jermaine said, interrupting my thoughts. "I've been waiting to meet you for months."

"Really?"

"Yeah. Manika's been talking about you and me hooking up for a while now. But our schedules never aligned. Finally, you're here in front of me, and I gotta say, her description didn't do you justice."

"Hold on. Let me stop you right there." I raised a hand, cutting him off before he could go any further. "I don't know what Manika told you, but I'm in a relationship. I have a man, and I'm not looking for anyone on the side. I don't know how you roll, but—"

"Wait, wait, wait," Jermaine interrupted, a smirk tugging at the corner of his lips. "I know you have a man. I'm not trying to be your side, dude. Like I said, Manika told me all about you. I just wanted to meet you because I know you work at the radio station. I'm producing a group, and I was hoping you could help get our single in rotation. That's all."

"Oh." My stomach twisted with embarrassment. I had completely misread the situation. "My bad. I didn't mean to come at you like that. I've just been going through a lot lately." I sighed, rubbing my temple.

Jermaine chuckled. "It's cool."

"If you have a copy of your CD, I can give it to my program director," I offered. "He does a new artist profile on his show. You can come in for an interview, and he'll play your song. Listeners call in and decide if it's a hit or miss."

Jermaine's face lit up. "Oh, yeah. That would be dope. That's exactly what we're looking for. Maybe you could help us get some local gigs, too. My group is good, we just want to get out there and get our music in front of the right people, you know?"

I glanced back toward the house. "So those guys in the living room—that's your group?"

"Yeah." He nodded. "They were all singing when I started working at the TV station, but they didn't have anyone managing their career. Since I can't sing, I stepped in to help. So far, we're in rotation in Atlanta, and we've played gigs in Birmingham and the Carolinas, but I'm always looking to put my guys in front of a bigger audience."

"I feel you," I said, giving him a small smile and beginning to relax into our conversation. "Look, I really want to apologize again for coming off like that. Like I said, I've got a lot going on."

"Nah, we're good," he reassured, shaking his head. A mischievous glint flashed in his eyes. "I gotta admit, though—"

I interrupted with an "I knew it" type of laugh. "I guess I assumed right, huh? I didn't mean to interrupt you but I knew there was something more to our chance meeting."

Jermaine flashed me a huge smile, showing off perfect rows of beautiful white teeth. At that moment I really looked into his eyes. What I saw was not a man out for just sex. There was something else going on in his mind. I was a bit taken aback because sex was normally what men led with when we first met. But there was something genuine about him that I didn't notice before and I was surprisingly intrigued. I apologized for coming off so harsh at first but the smile on his face and the look of sincerity in his eyes made me feel something I hadn't felt in a long time. Needed and wanted. Of course, I didn't want him to know that just the mere look he was giving me had softened my heart to him so quickly, so I had to maintain my composure.

"Now, see. How did the conversation go from me helping you get your group in front of my program director to—"

"Hey, now, let me interrupt you," he said, grabbing my hand. "I know what you're gonna say. Yo' girl filled me in on a few things about you and yes, my original goal was to talk with you about meeting the dude in programming at the station, but once Manika kept insisting that we talk and she showed me your picture, I *did* tell her I wanted to speak with you in person. Look, on the real . . . Ann, yo' boy, Kelly—"

"Kevin," I said, wondering just how much Manika told him and how he even knew his name, or a resemblance of his name.

"Yeah, Kevin. He don't know what he got. I'm not trying to diss ol' boy but dude trippin'."

"I'm not sure if I want to continue this conversation," I said, snatching my hand away. "I'm hosting under false pretenses and I don't appreciate you being so opinionated on a situation you really don't know anything about. I understand you and Manika are friends, but I hardly know you and if you're trying to gain something from me, this is not the way to do it," I continued with more force in my voice. "Are you perfect? Are you God's gift to women? Do you have all the answers? Have you ever committed seven years of your life to someone, trying to hold a relationship together while trying to hold yourself together?"

I heard the tremble in my voice and water began to well up in my eyes. I knew I had said enough and probably too much and needed to end the conversation before my emotions got the best of me. I also wasn't really sure how to feel about Manika sharing my business with Jermaine. It just made me wonder what kind of conversations they'd had. How many and how long?

I was full of emotions at this point. Hurt, anger, betrayal, everything was swirling around in my head because of what Jermaine said. The sad part about it was that I couldn't be mad at the truth. I could only be angry at the messenger, who just happened to be handsome and who also admitted to wanting me. Through all these emotions, I had to maintain my stoic composure. I briefly turned my head and looked towards the pond so Jermaine couldn't see a small tear fall from my face. I used the sleeve of my shirt to quickly wipe it away and turned back to face him.

"Ann, I don't want to upset you," Jermaine said, placing his hand on my cheek. "Let's just change the subject because I'm not here to spend time with a gorgeous woman and talk about some dude who's not treating her right. Listen," he continued, lowering his voice, so I could really hear the bass undertones of his speech. "We've already talked about business. I already told you that was my main goal. Since that is done, let me show you how a man treats a woman."

Something about the way he said that made my stomach clench. A slow, unexpected heat spread through my body. I wasn't sure why, but suddenly, I found myself hanging on his every word. My gaze drifted to his mouth—the shape of his lips, the way they moved, the flicker of his tongue. A thought crept in, uninvited. What would it feel like if his lips, his mouth, his tongue were on me?

"Hey, you okay?" Jermaine's voice snapped me out of my daze.

I blinked. "Um . . . yeah. I'm good." I cleared my throat. "You wanna go back inside?"

"Nah, we're good out here," he said, his gaze locked on me. "Besides, that spades game is getting too loud. I wanna be able to hear every word you have to say to me."

I don't know how I managed, but a smile began to form on my face. "You know if you really wanted to meet my program director, Keith, you could've just come to the station during business hours. He would've been more than happy to meet with you. Just admit it . . . you came all this way to flirt with me, didn't you?" I said coyly, trying to lighten the mood.

Jermaine leaned in slightly, his eyes dark and unreadable. "Nah . . . never that. You got a man and all. I don't wanna be your side dude."

"I know, right?" I teased, trying to play it cool.

"But . . ." His voice dropped an octave, thick with something unspoken. "I could be *something*."

The words hung between us, heavy and charged. Before I could process what was happening, he moved closer, his hands gripping my shoulders. In one fluid motion, he pulled me into a kiss.

I gasped against his lips, my mind screaming at me to stop. *This is wrong. You have a man.* But the moment his lips pressed against mine, soft and firm all at once, my body betrayed me. I resisted at first, but his grip was unyielding, his warmth intoxicating.

My struggle melted into surrender.

His hold softened, shifting from possession to tenderness. His lips moved with slow precision, coaxing a response from me, and I gave it to him. His mouth traveled down to my neck, his breath hot against my skin. My head lolled back, a soft "mmmm" escaping my lips before I could stop it.

I was in trouble.

And I didn't even care.

As his lips trailed down my neck, his breath sent a shiver through me. He moved closer to my ear and whispered, "Let me have you tonight."

My heart wanted to say no.

But the rest of me betrayed it.

"Yes," I breathed, the word slipping out before I could stop it.

Jermaine stood from the sofa on the balcony, his fingers lacing through mine as he led me inside. It felt surreal, as if I were floating. The sounds of laughter and conversation spilled from the living room, grounding me for just a moment. He walked to the bedroom door, gently pressing it shut before turning the lock with a quiet click.

I could have stopped this.

I could have told him to leave.

But I didn't.

Kevin's betrayal with Rhonda still haunted me, and maybe—just maybe—being with Jermaine would erase that pain, if only for a night.

I swallowed hard. "Jermaine . . ."

Before I could finish, his lips captured mine, his tongue sliding deep into my mouth, tasting me, claiming me. He pulled back just enough to strip off his T-shirt, revealing chiseled muscles and smooth, glistening skin. My fingertips traced his chest, firm yet warm beneath my touch.

His eyes burned into mine as he loosened his belt, slipping his pants off in one fluid motion. His boxer briefs clung to him, accentuating the undeniable evidence of his arousal. My breath caught in my throat.

When he finally removed his underwear, heat pooled between my thighs.

I lay back on the bed, the sound of Brianna and Manika's laughter echoing faintly in the background. If only they could see me now.

Jermaine climbed onto the bed, his strong hands starting at my ankles, kneading slow, deliberate circles as he worked his way up. My skin tingled beneath his touch. When he reached the waistband of my jeans, he unbuttoned them effortlessly and slid them down, his knuckles grazing my thighs, leaving a trail of fire in their wake.

Luckily, I had just shaved.

He lifted my shirt over my head, leaving me in only my bra and panties. Then he paused, eyes roaming over me like he was savoring every inch.

"Beautiful," he whispered.

His fingers slipped beneath the fabric of my panties, gliding over my wetness. I gasped, my hips instinctively rising to meet him. His touch sent electric waves through me, pushing me over the edge again and again.

And then he joined me.

The world blurred.

Time ceased to exist.

I lost myself in him.

Hours later, a knock at the door stirred us from our tangled sheets.

"Yo . . . Jay," a voice called from the other side. "We gotta hit the road. You know we got that photoshoot first thing in the morning."

Jermaine blinked, stretching lazily as a satisfied smile played on his lips.

"Aight, I'm coming." He sat up and reached for his clothes.

I watched as he dressed, still catching my breath, still trying to process what had just happened.

"Hey, Ann, I gotta go," he said, buttoning his pants. "Check this out; here's my number. Call me and let me know when you can set up something with me and the programming dude . . . or, you know, if you just wanna talk."

I raised a brow. "Well, I guess I need to give you my number then."

He smirked. "I already got yours."

"Oh?" I tilted my head. "You do?"

"Yeah, your girl Brianna gave it to me when she sent me the directions to your place." He winked. "I'll holla at you later."

Leaning in, he brushed a slow, lingering kiss against my lips before walking out the door.

I slipped into my bathrobe and crept into the living room, where Brianna and Manika were sprawled across the couch, fast asleep. The guys were making their way out, and I murmured a quiet goodbye before retreating to my bedroom.

Sliding back beneath the covers, I stared at the ceiling, my body still humming, my thoughts whirling.

CHAPTER 11

CHANGING THE DIAL

The next two weeks dragged on as if I were a child eagerly awaiting Christmas morning—agonizingly slow. I wasn't one to sit idly, but I chose to use my time off to clear my head and figure out what I wanted to do with the rest of my life. The future I had once mapped out had come to an abrupt halt, largely due to Kevin and Rhonda constantly creeping into my thoughts. If someone had told me a few years ago, fresh out of college, that Kevin and I wouldn't be together, I would've laughed in their face. But here I was, questioning everything I once believed was unshakable. No matter how badly I wanted to trust that Kevin wasn't seeing Rhonda, certain things didn't add up. How did she even have his work number? Why did she feel comfortable enough to invite him to her house first thing in the morning? And why hadn't he told me any of this? My mind was overwhelmed with questions that I couldn't suppress, no matter how hard I tried.

The night I spent with Jermaine had stirred up even more doubts—about Kevin, my job, everything. Although I didn't have to see Rhonda anymore, the humiliation of what I'd done at the station still lingered. How was I supposed to explain leaping over the receptionist's desk? I was sure my coworkers had already drawn their conclusions, but I wasn't eager to face them. Jermaine and I had been talking every day since that night, which made me uneasy. I couldn't afford to fall for him, not while I was so vulnerable, but it felt good to be with someone who didn't make me question everything.

The day before I was scheduled to return to work, I decided I needed some time alone. Not with the girls, not to meet a guy—just me. I grabbed my keys, determined to clear my head, and headed to the dollar movie theatre down the street. I never used to do things like that on my own, always feeling awkward about going to a movie or sitting in a restaurant alone. But today, I didn't care. I needed space, and since it was matinee time, I figured the odds of running into someone I knew were slim.

As soon as I stepped out of my car, I heard someone call my name. "Angela Parkens . . . well, well, well. How are you?"

I turned to see Frank Townsend, a big grin spread across his face. Frank Townsend was a successful businessman who owned the rival urban station, Townsend Communications. He'd been trying to recruit me for years, ever since I started winning local advertising awards, always joking that I was stealing his clients because they liked my work better.

"Mr. Townsend," I greeted, trying to mask my surprise. "Fancy running into you here. How are you?"

"I'm good. And you're looking good, as usual."

At fifty, he was still a flirt, but I had to admit—he was brilliant at what he did. I let out a polite laugh.

"Catching a movie?" I asked.

"We're having a staff meeting here. One of our clients lets us use their conference room." He grinned. "Though I probably shouldn't be telling you that. Trade secrets and all. But seriously, when are you going to come to work for me? We'd love to have you."

I hesitated for a moment. I wasn't someone who believed in coincidences—everything happened for a reason, and maybe this was the opportunity I needed.

"You know what, Mr. Townsend?" I said, collecting my thoughts.

"Frank, please. Call me Frank."

"Okay, Frank. I'd like to sit down and talk about that. Seriously. I think it's time for a change."

He smiled broadly.

"That's what I like to hear! Here's my card. Call my secretary and set up an appointment for next week."

He handed me his card, shook my hand, and headed inside. I stood there, staring at the card in disbelief. Leaving the station hadn't been something I'd seriously considered until now, but suddenly, it felt like the right move. The next day, I walked into work, bracing myself for the mountain of tasks that awaited me after two weeks off. Normally, even after a long weekend, my desk would be overflowing with work. But when I stepped into my office, I was met with an empty desk— except for a memo. Curious, I picked it up. Keith wanted to hold a staff meeting at three. I had barely settled in when I heard a knock on my door.

"Morning," Keith said as he stepped inside.

"Morning," I replied, forcing a smile.

"I'm glad to see you back. We tried to stay on top of things while you were gone so you wouldn't come back to a mess."

"Thanks, I appreciate it." I tried to sound genuine, but for some reason, talking to him irritated me that morning.

"You okay?" he asked, eyeing me with concern.

"Yeah, I'm good. Why?"

"You just seem . . . off." He stepped further in and closed the door. "Look, I know you've been dealing with some personal stuff, and I hope you used these two weeks to sort it out. But we've got the ratings book coming up. We need to be at the top of our game."

"I'm fine," I said, avoiding eye contact as tears started to well up. "I'll be ready."

"Good. I'll see you at the meeting." With that, he left. I looked down at the file in my hands, fighting to keep it together. But when I blinked, tears fell onto the pages, blurring the ink. I grabbed a tissue and wiped my eyes. It wasn't like me to cry at work—what the hell was going on? I glanced at the clock—9:45 a.m.

Reaching into my purse, I pulled out Frank Townsend's card and dialed the number. His secretary answered, and I quickly set up an appointment for next week. Maybe this was the change I needed.

That night, I sat on the balcony, waiting for Kevin to come home. I glanced at the patio sofa, remembering the night with Jermaine, and smiled. I hadn't spoken to him in a few days, so I decided to give him a quick call before Kevin got home. Jermaine picked up on the first ring.

"What up?"

"Hey, what are you up to?"

"I was just thinking about you. Glad you called. I've got some news—guess what?"

"You sound excited. What's up?"

"I've got a meeting with your program director, Keith."

"Oh yeah? Finally getting that music meeting?"

"Nah, this is about a DJ gig."

"A DJ gig?" I repeated, confused. Jermaine had mentioned he worked in television and managed a music group, but DJing was news to me.

"Yeah, I sent Keith a few of my mixes, and he liked them. They're thinking about bringing me in for Saturday nights."

"That's great!" I said, trying to match his excitement.

"You know what that means, right? More time for you and me to . . . reconnect."

"Stop it," I laughed, blushing. "You're gonna get me in trouble. Listen, I can't talk long—Kevin should be home soon. But I have to wish you luck with the DJ thing. Let me know how it goes."

"I will. But listen, Ann. I've gotta tell you something."

"What now? Did they offer you my job, too?" I joked.

"No, nothing like that. When me and you started this thing, whatever you may want to call it, I kinda felt like we had an understanding. I knew you had some things to sort out wit ol' boy and I wasn't really looking for anything serious either."

"Yeah," I said, hoping the conversation wasn't about to take a turn for the worse. Jermaine had been pressing me more and more lately to break up with Kevin and I was really tired of talking about it. I thought I'd made that sentiment clear in our last few conversations.

"But I'm tired of playing second fiddle to this guy," he said.

"Woah . . . wait . . . why do we need to keep having this same conversation? Jermaine, I love talking to you. We have wonderful conversations and I do enjoy the time we spend together but . . ." I hesitated. "I'm with Kevin." As the words came out of my mouth, I didn't believe them and I'm sure Jermaine knew I wasn't confident in what I just said either.

"Ann, you've been talking to me about that dude since the first night we met, and it's obvious he's messing around. He's not the one for you. You caught him at Rhonda's place, and he still talked his way out of it. I don't know how you can trust him."

"Jermaine, I'm not doing this with you. I love Kevin, and if he says nothing's going on, I believe him. I'm not leaving him unless I see him with her myself." I slammed the phone down just as Kevin walked into the bedroom.

"Damn, what was that all about?" he asked, peeling off his uniform.

"Oh, that was Keith," I lied. "Just work stuff."

"Babe, I had a long day. I'm gonna hit the shower and go to bed, okay?" He gave me a peck on the cheek before disappearing into the bathroom.

As I listened to the water running, Jermaine's words echoed in my head. Was I being naive about this entire situation with Rhonda and Kevin? I was an educated woman with a career on an upward trajectory. I had a lot going for myself. Kevin and I made a wonderful team. Once he was done getting his master's degree and opened his barbershop, we would be on our way to do all the things we had talked about. Marriage, kids, buying real estate, all the things. He was a good man for me and I just couldn't bring myself to believe that he would betray me in a big way, not again. I'd talked to Jermaine about my relationship with Kevin, but he didn't really understand. He didn't understand the years Kevin and I had shared, the talks and promises we'd made to each other, and the love we shared. Yes, there had been heartache, but we were past that now. Weren't we?

Another thought crossed my mind. Jermaine's insistence on my leaving Kevin was becoming more and more persistent. I could clearly tell he was starting to develop deep feelings for me but I didn't think he would be so bold as to keep suggesting for me to leave my relationship. Was he my karma? I liked Jermaine and he was a welcome distraction from all the issues in my life right now but the last thing I needed was for *him* to become an issue. I needed to try to keep the peace with Jermaine as much as I could, so I would need to smooth things over with him when he came to the station to meet with Keith; I'd see him and talk with him then. I knew he probably didn't appreciate me ending our conversation so abruptly.

Hopefully, he realized that I wasn't leaving Kevin and he and I could just continue to be good friends. Hopefully.

CHAPTER 12

SIGNALS CROSSED

Jermaine walked into the station, looking as good as ever. He wasn't in a suit, but the rough edge of his outfit made me want to leap into his arms right then and there. He wore a simple white T-shirt, a gold chain with a diamond-encrusted "J" charm, dark denim jeans, and crisp, clean sneakers. *Damn*, I thought, my eyes tracing over him. I knew his interview was at noon, so I made sure to be at the front desk. We hadn't spoken in days, and I needed to remind him that I was still thinking about him—and that we needed to talk. He walked in and threw me a wink.

"Hey, beautiful."

"Hey yourself," I replied, my voice betraying a little too much excitement.

Just then, Keith walked out of his office and headed our way. He greeted Jermaine in a friendly, casual manner. As they walked back to Keith's office, I couldn't help but feel a twinge of doubt. Jermaine, possibly working at the same station? It wasn't like I wanted him out of my life on the side, but how long could I keep it hidden? Everyone at the station thought Kevin and I were the perfect couple, all smiles on the outside. Little did they know that it was Kevin who pushed me to leap over that desk at Rhonda.

Lost in thought, I made my way back to my office, trying to refocus. I had a big meeting with Mr. Townsend, and the question of whether I was going to leave the station and head across town hung over me like a storm cloud. All I knew for certain was that I needed a serious change, either professionally or personally.

Hours later, Jermaine and Keith emerged from the office. I'd been trying to get work done, but my mind was swimming with everything. Jermaine's voice pulled me out of my daze.

"Hey . . . you. Got dinner plans?" he asked, stepping into my office.

I glanced at the clock. It was already thirty minutes past four in the evening. Where had the time gone? I hadn't done anything productive, and Kevin still wasn't picking up his phone, either at work or on his cell.

"No plans. Didn't realize it was that late."

"Well, since you're free, how about we grab a drink? You can show me around the city, you know, all the best places to live."

"What?"

He grinned. "Yo' boy got the job. I'll be mixing live on the weekends. Keith's even hooking me up with a few live club remotes."

"Well, look at you! Congrats! I guess we should celebrate. How about The Spotlight? It's a new club that just opened downtown. I've been a few times. They have a decent happy hour and they fry their wings hard, so you know they're good. They've got fish too. That's cool with you?"

"Yeh, I can go for some fish."

"I could also probably introduce you to the owner. He owes me a favor and I'm sure if I vouch for you, he will give you a chance to DJ on Saturday nights. The house DJ just moved to Memphis and they don't have anybody right now." I saw a slight smile on Jermaine's face. I hoped this would placate him for the moment, so that we could get back to normal and forget about our last conversation.

"Damn . . . thanks for the hookup. You really know how to look out for your boy."

"It's no problem. Let me finish up here and I'll meet you in the front lobby in about thirty minutes."

"Aight, cool." he said and gave me a wink and headed to the lobby.

Once I knew he was out of earshot, I picked up my office phone and tried Kevin once again. This time, his phone didn't ring at all. The voicemail came on as soon as I was done dialing the number. His phone was turned off. At this point, my eyes began to water. The only thing I could do was just sit at my desk and stare at the wall. I thought to myself, *Not today, Ann. Not today*. After about twenty minutes of just sitting and staring at nothing, I regained my composure. I grabbed my purse from my chair and headed to the front lobby where Jermaine was waiting. I needed a break from the chaos in my mind. Jermaine was the perfect distraction, and I promised myself not to think about Kevin for the rest of the night.

I hopped into my car and told Jermaine to follow. When we pulled into the club's parking lot, it was packed. I found a spot near the door, and Jermaine pulled in behind me. He walked up and grabbed my hand, but I quickly pulled away. We stood there, locked in an awkward gaze.

"What's that about?" Jermaine asked, his voice low but firm.

I sighed, keeping my eyes on the sidewalk ahead. "Come on, you know people know me here."

"Oh, so what? They know you're still with that nigga?"

"Jermaine . . ."

"Nah, it's cool." He shoved his hands into his pockets. "Let's go inside."

This wasn't how I wanted the night to go.

We stepped into the club, the bass from the speakers vibrating through my chest. The air smelled of sweat, liquor, and expensive perfume. As we made our way to the bar, I felt eyes on me—people whispering, watching.

"Angela P!" the bartender called out, his grin wide. "Where you been, girl? Ain't seen you in a minute."

"Hey, D, what's up?" I forced a smile. "Just been laying low. Good to see you." I gestured toward Jermaine. "This is my friend Jermaine. He's a new DJ at the station. Just showing him around the scene." My words were quick, too quick, as if I needed to establish an explanation of why I was here with Jermaine before D could ask the wrong questions.

Jermaine shook hands with the bartender, but I caught the way D looked at me—like he saw right through my deflection.

"You know if David's around?" I continued. "I was hoping that he and Jermaine could meet, since he's looking for a house DJ. Maybe they could talk about some business."

"Yeah, I think he's in the back," D replied. "I'll get him."

"Thanks," I said.

The night went smoothly after that. Jermaine and David hit it off, talking music and industry moves, and for a while, I could breathe. We laughed and shared drinks, and for a moment, things felt normal.

Until Jermaine asked the question.

"You mind if I crash at your place instead of driving back to Atlanta?"

My heart stopped.

"My place?"

"Yeah . . . unless that's a problem."

I hesitated. I didn't want Jermaine to think he wasn't welcome at my place but I also didn't know where Kevin was and I certainly didn't want any chance meetings between them.

"Nah, it's cool," I finally said after a few minutes of awkward silence. "It's late, and Atlanta's a long drive. You can crash on the couch."

Jermaine gave me a knowing look.

"The couch? Yeah . . . right." He smirked.

As many times as Jermaine had been to my apartment, he had never slept on the couch. Hell, I had never offered him the couch.

I swallowed hard. I wanted him in my bed, wanted to feel his body against mine again, but the risk was too high. Kevin was unaccounted for, and if he showed up, I'd have no explanation for Jermaine being in my apartment. On the other hand, Kevin was once again in the wind. Not returning my phone calls and not picking up at work. Wherever he was, I was sure he realized that I was trying to reach him or that he should at least check in with me. That's the courteous thing to do when you're in a relationship. Especially one like ours, with so many tears, rips, and questionable events.

While deep in my thoughts, the tears that started to stream down my face dried up and the hurt I was feeling slowly turned into anger. How dare he? All the things we went through while in college with Alicia. The promise he made to me when he asked me to abort our baby to save his *good guy* reputation. Can you imagine if everyone knew that he had gotten two women pregnant at the same time, and all before graduating from college? The audacity he now had, to allow even the slightest thought of infidelity to creep into my mind—and with Rhonda of all people. He should have been doing all he could to calm my thoughts. Prove to me that he was a man of his word and not do anything that would jeopardize our future together. If he did show up at my apartment and Jermaine was there, so what? I was the one who should be asking all the questions, not him. Besides, I paid the rent. Kevin had not offered any monetary assistance. Not that I had asked for any, but I shouldn't have had to. I looked up at Jermaine and gave a slight smile.

"Hey, you ready to go?" I asked. "It's getting late and I'm getting sleepy." He nodded at me and we stood up from the table and headed towards the door.

On the way home, I tried calling Kevin again. No answer.

When we arrived at my apartment, I parked in my usual space and Jermaine found a spot on the other side of the parking lot. I got out of my car and did a quick scan of the area to see if I could see Kevin's car. One last ditch effort, I guess, to tell Jermaine he couldn't stay, even though I really wanted him to. Some part of me was hoping that Kevin was at my place asleep and that's why he hadn't answered my calls, but there was no sign of Kevin's Acura. We walked up the steps to my front door and I could feel Jermaine's eyes on my body as my heels clicked and met with the pavement below. Once we got inside, I grabbed pillows and a comforter from the linen closet.

"Okay, here you go. Should be comfy on the couch."

Jermaine smirked, stepping closer. "You really expect me to sleep on the couch?" His voice was low, teasing, but there was a hunger in his eyes. He slid his hands up my arms, fingers pressing gently into my shoulders. "Let me hold you tonight."

His touch was electric, his presence overwhelming. I wanted to say yes.

But—

"Look, Jermaine . . . you being here is risky. Kevin's probably on his way, and I'll have to explain why you're on the couch—"

Before I could finish, he kissed me.

And just like that, my resolve crumbled.

He lifted me effortlessly into his arms and carried me to the bedroom, laying me down as if I were the most precious thing he had ever touched.

And then we lost ourselves in each other.

His body moved against mine, his rhythm sending me over the edge again and again. I clung to him, desperate to forget Kevin, to forget everything but this moment.

Then—

Keys rattled at the door.

My stomach dropped.

"Jermaine, hurry! Get dressed and get to the couch," I whispered frantically, scrambling for my robe.

He gave me a look—one filled with frustration—but he obeyed, throwing on his clothes and slipping under the comforter just as Kevin walked in.

"Hey, baby," I said quickly, moving toward him, and wrapping him in a hug before he could take in the scene.

Kevin barely hugged me back, his eyes locked on Jermaine. His expression darkened.

"Who's this?"

Panic shot through me.

"Baby, I tried to call you. This is Jermaine, the new DJ at the station. He had some club meetings and needed to crash before heading back to Atlanta."

Jermaine stood, extending a hand. "What's up, man?"

Kevin's jaw clenched. His eyes flickered between me and Jermaine before he scoffed.

"I don't give a fuck who he is. What is he doing in my apartment?"

I realized then Jermaine had been waiting for a moment like this. He only needed a small amount of ammunition to confront Kevin. No matter what Kevin said during their interaction tonight, from this point on, it was enough to make Jermaine snap.

Jermaine stepped forward.

"Yo, nigga, who the fuck are you talking to?"

I jumped between them, pushing my hands against their chests. "Y'all need to chill! This is crazy. Kevin, Jermaine's just crashing on the couch, okay? Nothing more."

"Nah, fuck that." Kevin's voice was cold, final. "This nigga needs to leave."

Then, without another word, he disappeared into the bedroom.

I turned to Jermaine, my heart racing. "Look, Jermaine . . . I think it's best if you go." My voice shook.

He stared at me, his expression unreadable.

"After everything?" His voice was tight. "I love you, Ann. You're still gonna fuck with that nigga?"

The words slammed into me.

"You . . . love me?" I whispered.

"I do." His voice was raw, filled with something I wasn't ready to process. "And you know damn well dat nigga don't love you. He's fucking around with Rhonda, and you know it."

I froze.

"You got a decision to make," he continued, stepping back toward the door. "Either you tell him what's up, or I will."

With that, he grabbed his things and left.

The second the door shut, Kevin walked back in.

"So that nigga's gone, huh?"

"Yeah," I murmured, my mind spinning.

I was in deep now. Jermaine had said he loved me. And worse? He was ready to tell Kevin everything.

My escape plan was clear.

Mr. Townsend's offer couldn't come soon enough.

CHAPTER 13

A SEAT AT THE TABLE

I rose early, as I always did, to prepare Kevin's usual breakfast—grits, cheesy scrambled eggs, and crispy bacon. Sausages had never been his thing. Back in college, he'd mentioned that he liked his grits with a splash of milk stirred in, so ever since, I made sure to add that little touch of milk and cheese—like a ritual. But today wasn't quite the same. I had to stay focused. This was the day of my big meeting with Mr. Townsend. For months, he'd tried to get me to his stations, and every time, I had turned him down. But now, with Jermaine joining my station and after the tense meeting he'd had with Kevin, I knew the time had come for me to make my move.

After seeing Kevin off to work, I headed to my closet to pick an outfit, my mind already running through the conversation ahead. I'd called Keith earlier to tell him I'd be coming in after lunch, citing a "doctor's appointment." No need for him to know the truth. My meeting with Mr. Townsend was set for 10:30 that morning. I chose my sleek black suit, pulled my hair into a neat bun, grabbed my attaché case, and stepped out.

Half an hour later, I walked toward the Townsend Communications receptionist desk with a measured calm.

"Good morning, welcome to Townsend Communications. How may I assist you?" a young lady greeted with a polished smile. She was probably in her late twenties and sat behind a large glass desk with the words Townsend Communications etched on the front. This setup was certainly more appealing than KIBB. I was already impressed at what I saw. The receptionist seemed pleasant but I wondered, if we worked together, how long it would be before *she* tried to sleep Kevin.

"Good morning," I said, returning her smile. "I'm Angela Parkens. I have an appointment with Mr. Townsend."

"Yes, Ms. Parkens, he's expecting you. Please, go right in," she invited with a professional gesture toward the double doors to her left.

I gave an appreciative nod and turned towards the two closed doors. Although they were only a few feet from where I was standing, they seemed miles away. Whatever happened on the other side of these doors would change my life forever. I approached the door, took a deep breath, and knocked.

"Come on in, Ann," Mr. Townsend's familiar voice called out.

I turned the knob and entered, greeted by Mr. Townsend sitting at a conference table with two other gentlemen, who immediately stood and extended their hands.

"Ms. Parkens, this is Derrick West, our program director for the urban stations, and Rick Hamilton, our urban consultant from

Dallas," Mr. Townsend introduced, his tone confident, as though introducing a trusted team.

"Good morning, gentlemen," I greeted, shaking their hands firmly. "It's a pleasure to meet you both."

Mr. Hamilton smiled warmly. "We've heard a lot about you, Ms. Parkens."

"And let me tell you," Derrick added, "It's tough competing with you in the same market. The clients rave about your commercials. We're excited about the possibility of working with you."

I smiled modestly, but inside, I felt a surge of pride.

"Thank you, gentleman," I finally said. All three of these men towered over me. I had to make sure my posture was straight so that I would convey a strong presence. Even though Mr. Townsend said they've been following my work for years and they were familiar with me, I needed to come across as a woman who was about business. It's times like these that I needed to channel my mother. Although she was absent for most of my childhood, her voice was never far from me—"Men will try to turn your strength into a weakness. In a room full of them, don't shrink; speak like you've got the mic, even when they don't hand it to you."

Her absence hurt, but her lessons became my armor—and in every pitch, every late-night edit, every boardroom full of men trying to talk over me, her voice kept me standing tall.

"Please, let's all take a seat," Mr. Townsend said, gesturing toward the table. Without wasting time, he got straight to business. "Ann, we've been eager to have this conversation for quite some time. I'm glad you finally agreed to meet with us."

"Well," I began, keeping my tone measured, "I owe it to myself to explore any potential opportunities. Your stations have a strong reputation both in this market and regionally, and I'm open to seeing what the future holds."

"We certainly hope so," Derrick added. "We could really use someone of your caliber to take our stations to the next level."

Mr. Townsend leaned forward slightly, his voice taking on a more serious tone.

"Derrick has been offered a general manager position at a station in Orlando. It's a top 50 market, and I've encouraged him to take it."

I turned to Derrick. "Well, congratulations are definitely in order, I see," I said sincerely.

"Thank you," he replied with a smile. "I wasn't sure if that was the move I needed to make but after Frank and I talked and he gave me the okay, I decided what the hell," Derrick said with a shrug. "I mean, it's Florida. Come on, man, the weather . . . the women . . ." All the men let out a laugh.

I glanced around at all three men and they seemed to laugh even louder at Derrick's reference about the women. Probably thinking about the skimpy dresses and barely there shorts these women may wear, trying to escape the warm weather. I was a bit uncomfortable but made sure not to display it. I mustered a brief smile and cleared my throat, hoping to remind them that a woman was indeed in the room with them.

"Uh, yeh, back to business," Mr. Townsend finally continued. "With Derrick moving on, that leaves us with a significant gap in programming, and we want you to fill it," he said, pointing at me.

"So, Ms. Parkens, we'd like to offer you the position of program director for our urban stations."

For a moment, I was speechless. Program director? That wasn't at all what I had anticipated. I was honestly stunned. I walked into that meeting thinking they wanted to discuss the production manager role—I had even rehearsed a few modest lines of appreciation even though I knew they had been following my work for some time. But when they said *program director*, I just sat there for a second, blinking. It felt surreal. I mean, that was a major leadership position, shaping the entire sound and identity of the station.

"As you already know, we've been watching how you handled the creative strategy and team dynamics for months at KIBB. We want you here, Ann. We're prepared to offer you a very competitive benefits package," Mr. Townsend explained. "This includes a 401k, full benefits, and double your current salary. You'd oversee ten on-air staff members and help guide the station's new direction. Right now, we're too male-dominated, and we've been missing out on the demographic that drives spending—our female audience. We believe a female program director would give us the perfect edge, and you're exactly the woman we need."

My mind raced as he said the title once again: program director. The offer threw everything into a different perspective. This wasn't just a step up—it was a leap. I never imagined I'd be in a position to choose between playing it safe and taking a bold risk. But here I was, with an unexpected door wide open, and for once, I wasn't afraid to walk through it.

"Well, gentlemen," I finally said after taking it all in but still trying to remain calm. "I certainly appreciate your confidence in my abilities. "I have to say, coming from the production side and moving into programming is a big jump. My instincts and ability to—"

"Ann, you don't need to sell yourself to us," Mr. Hamilton chimed in. "We've seen your work in this market for a long time. We'd be remiss if we didn't offer you this opportunity. You understand radio and, more importantly, this market."

I sat there, my thoughts tumbling over each other, struggling to formulate a response. This offer was far beyond what I had imagined.

Mr. Townsend, sensing my surprise, gave me a reassuring smile.

"We understand this might be overwhelming, Ann. Take the weekend to think it over. Let us know your decision first thing Monday morning."

"Thank you," I managed to say. "I really appreciate the offer, and yes, I'd like some time to consider it. I'll give you my answer on Monday."

With that, I stood, shaking hands with everyone before heading out of the office. The moment I stepped into the privacy of my car, I let out a triumphant scream. I didn't need the weekend to think it over—I already knew my answer. I just needed to discuss it with Kevin.

That evening, Kevin arrived home earlier than usual. Without a word, he walked straight to the shower, a routine that had become disturbingly common between us. I barely gave it a second thought—until the phone rang.

"Hello?"

"Hey, sexy," Jermaine's voice purred through the line.

I lowered my voice, irritation creeping in. "Why are you calling me now? You know Kevin's here."

"Yeah, whatever. Fuck that nigga."

I clenched my jaw. "What do you want, Jermaine?"

"I just wanted to let you know I found a place. Stopped by the station earlier to see if you wanted to come check it out, but they said you'd already left. Should be all moved in by the end of the month."

"That's great, Jermaine. Now, I really have to go."

"By the way, I ran into your girl at the station today."

I frowned. "My girl? What are you talking about?"

"Rhonda? That's what she said her name was. And I thought, damn, so this is the chick ol' boy's messin' with? Yeh, she said she was there picking up her last paycheck. Looks like she's leaving the station. Anyway, we had a real good conversation . . ."

"Jermaine! You didn't tell her you knew me, did you?"

"Small world, isn't it," he said ignoring my question. "Turns out we have a lot in common. I'm actually meeting her for dinner tonight so we can talk further about the things we have in common. She seems pretty cool."

"You're having dinner with that bitch?"

"Ann, you know I want you, but you're still hung up on dude. I mean, I was ready to tell him about us, but you made it clear that wasn't what you wanted. Don't worry, I'll keep quiet about us. Have a good night, baby."

Before I could respond, he hung up.

Kevin emerged from the bathroom, a towel slung low around his waist, water still dripping from his skin. He walked over, kissed me on the cheek, and playfully smacked my ass.

"Who was that?" he asked casually.

"Oh, just Brianna," I replied evenly. "She wanted me to hang out with her and Manika tonight, but I told her I wasn't feeling up to it. Besides, I'd rather be here with you. It's not often we get to spend a whole evening together."

"Okay, babe. You know I'm beat from work, so I'll probably just knock out early. Why don't you make some popcorn? I'm gonna change into my pajamas and meet you in the bedroom."

I busied myself in the kitchen, the rhythmic pop of kernels breaking the thick silence pressing in on me.

Walking into the bedroom, I handed Kevin the bowl and slid into the bed beside him as he flipped through channels.

"Hey…I need to talk to you about something," I started cautiously.

"Yeah, what's up, babe?" Kevin said, throwing a few pieces of popcorn in his mouth and flipping through the channels on the TV.

"I had a meeting with Mr. Townsend today over at Townsend Communications."

Kevin's eyes stayed glued to the TV; he was barely registering my words.

"Oh yeah? They've been trying to get you over there for a while," he finally muttered.

"They offered me a job . . . Program director of their urban stations. Isn't that great?"

"Mmmhmm . . . yeah, that's great."

"I told them I'd think it over and get back to them on Monday. What do you think?"

"Do what you want, babe. Whatever you decide is fine with me. Here, take the remote. I'm going to sleep." He handed me the remote without even glancing at me, rolling over and drifting off almost immediately.

And that was it. No "Wow, babe, that's amazing," no "I'm proud of you," not even a smile. Just a sleepy mumble and his back to me. Like I'd told him I'd picked up milk on the way home, not that I'd been handed the keys to a major role I'd worked my ass off to earn.

I brooded as I lay there in the dark, blinking up at the ceiling, my excitement folding in on itself like a paper crane in reverse. This was supposed to be one of those moments. A milestone. Something we'd toast to, talk about, celebrate. I thought he'd see it—see *me*. But all I could hear was the steady rhythm of his breathing, already deepening into sleep, and the echo of my own silence stretching out in the dark beside him.

Funny how loud nothing can be.

I stayed up for hours, aimlessly flicking through channels, trying to find something to focus on. But my thoughts kept circling back to Kevin and the growing coldness between us. Eventually, exhaustion claimed me, and I dozed off.

When I woke up the next morning, I found Kevin still lying beside me, staring blankly at the ceiling. His jaw was set tight, and I could feel the tension radiating off him. I knew this was the moment—we couldn't keep pretending everything was fine.

"Morning," I said cautiously, propping myself up on my elbow. He didn't turn to look at me.

"Morning," he muttered, his voice flat and distant. My heart pounded in my chest as I searched for the right words.

"We need to talk," I finally managed to say. Kevin sighed, running a hand over his face.

"About what, Ann?"

"About us. About how things are," I blurted out. "I feel like we're on two different pages, and it scares me."

He rolled over to face me, his eyes tired. "You're overthinking this," he said dismissively. "Things are fine. We're just going through a rough patch. It happens."

"But it doesn't feel fine," I insisted, frustration rising in my voice. "Lately, I feel like I don't even know you. We used to talk about everything, but now it's like you're a stranger in our own bed." Kevin's face hardened.

"So now I'm the problem? Is that it? Just because we're not glued to each other every second doesn't mean something's wrong."

"It's not about being glued to each other," I shot back, sitting up straighter. "It's about feeling connected. Lately, it feels like we're just going through the motions."

He threw off the covers, sitting on the edge of the bed with his back to me.

"You always do this, Ann. Overanalyze every little thing until there's nothing left but doubt."

I felt a sting at his words but pushed through it.

"Maybe because I care enough to want to fix things before they fall apart," I said, my voice breaking. "You're acting like I'm making this up, but I know you feel it too."

He stood up, running a hand through his hair, and turned to face me, his eyes icy. "Maybe we rushed into this," he said bluntly. "Maybe we're not as ready for this as we thought."

His words hit me like a punch to the gut. I sat there, stunned and reeling, as the truth of his statement settled in the room like a fog. This was the reality I had been trying to avoid, the one I was terrified of facing.

"Maybe," I whispered, my voice trembling. "But what do we do about it?"

For a moment, he just stared at me, his face unreadable. Then he shook his head.

"I don't know," he muttered, looking away.

The room felt colder as he walked out, leaving me alone with the echoes of our broken conversation. I lay back down in bed and pulled the covers over me as tears began to fall. The weight of it all—the lies, the deceit—pressed heavily on my chest. The only thing I knew for certain was that I had to leave him.

CHAPTER 14

LOVE AND AMBITION

Monday morning arrived faster than I had anticipated, and before I knew it, I was heading to work. Despite my best efforts to focus, the last thing on my mind was the job. Mr. Townsend and his team were waiting for an answer regarding the program director position. I had looming production deadlines from the previous week, thanks to leaving early on Friday. I hadn't had a real conversation with Kevin about the offer from Townsend Communications. He'd seemed distant all weekend, and to complicate things further, Jermaine had been calling the house non-stop. I ignored his calls, refusing to pick up the phone. All these decisions weighed heavily on me—about my career, about Kevin, about Jermaine—and I knew I had to take action soon. I couldn't keep living in this drama.

As I walked from the parking lot toward the station, I spotted Jermaine pulling up in the station van, parking right by the front door. Avoiding him wasn't an option now. I wasn't sure what to say, but I steeled myself.

"What's up, Ann?" Jermaine greeted me, his tone flat—not the usual warm welcome I was accustomed to from him.

I forced myself to respond.

"Hey. Where have you been this morning?"

"Well, if you'd answered my calls over the weekend, you'd know. Today's my first day. Keith scheduled me for a morning remote at that new breakfast spot down the street. He said he was going to talk to you about putting together a promo since the station's covering the event all week. Oh, and I need intro drops for my show."

"You're all about business this morning," I observed, noticing the shift in his demeanor.

"Isn't that all you want from me?" he shot back. "Look . . ." He paused, his eyes locking with mine. "Ann, let's cut the crap. I want you. And I know you want me too, but for whatever reason, you're still holding on to that guy Kevin. You know I had dinner with Rhonda the other night, right?"

I glared at him.

"Why are you hanging out with her now?"

"She's cool with me. I've got no reason to dislike her."

"Yeah . . . okay." I couldn't hide my disgust.

Jermaine shrugged.

"I'm tired of going back and forth on this. Give me a chance. I can make you happy. How about I come over tonight, and we can talk things through?"

I knew exactly where that conversation would lead. Sex. Great sex, but not the kind I needed, not while I was still trying to figure things out with Kevin. But instead of saying no, I surprised myself.

"Sure, come over. How does seven o'clock sound?"

Jermaine smirked.

"Sounds like we're both in for a good night." He closed the doors to the station van and disappeared inside.

I wasn't worried about Kevin; I knew he'd be at work. Jermaine coming over would give me a chance to vent about everything, especially since Brianna and Manika were tired of hearing me talk about it. They had both told me to let the whole situation go, to leave Kevin behind. But they just didn't get it—it wasn't that simple.

As I made my way into the station, something felt different. Normally, when I walked through those doors, I felt like I belonged— like this was my space. Today, though, I felt like a stranger. The walls seemed colder, the air stifling, and I couldn't shake the feeling that I needed to leave.

By the time I reached my office and sat at my desk, I knew what that feeling meant. It was time. A sign that I needed to call Mr. Townsend and accept the offer. And that's exactly what I did.

Mr. Townsend's excitement was palpable over the phone, his enthusiasm infectious as he welcomed me aboard.

After hanging up, I sat at my computer and began typing my resignation letter. Luckily, I hadn't signed a non-compete agreement, so I could give my two weeks' notice without any issues. If I had signed one, I would've had to sit out for six months before joining another station in the area. That was a small blessing.

Once I had printed my resignation letter and proofread it, I made my way to Keith's office. My heart raced a little as I knocked on the door.

"Come in," Keith's voice called from inside. I peeked my head through the door.

"Hey, you got a minute?"

"Yeah, come on in." I stepped inside and sat down across from him. With a small, bittersweet smile, I handed him the letter.

"Ann . . . what's this?" Keith asked, glancing over the resignation letter.

"Keith, I love working here and I appreciate everything you've done for me. You took a chance on me right out of college, and I've learned so much. But I feel like it's time for me to move on. I've been offered a programming job at Townsend Communications, and I've accepted."

"Well, damn," Keith said, stunned but smiling. He blinked, surprised, but nodded slowly. I could tell he wasn't shocked by *why*, just by *when*. "I knew they were interested in you, but I didn't realize they were offering you the program director position. West must be moving on?"

"Yeah, he got a gig in Orlando."

"Wow, Ann. I don't know what else to say except congratulations. You deserve this."

Keith stood up from behind his desk, walked over, and gave me an unexpected hug. "You're like a daughter to me. I know you've been going through some personal stuff, but you'll get through it. If you ever need anything from me, don't hesitate to call. This couldn't happen to a nicer person."

"Thank you, Keith. It really means a lot to hear that."

I left Keith's office after a few more pleasantries and headed to the production room. The fluorescent lights in the studio never got any softer, no matter how many years I'd spent under them. Today, they felt especially harsh. Maybe it was the weight of everything I had to do, or maybe it was just the clarity that comes when you've finally said the thing you've been carrying for months: *I'm leaving.*

I was flying through edits like a machine. Spots for next week's drive-time ads. A last-minute re-cut for a moody late-night segment that was going to need just the right bed of ambient jazz. I bounced between software windows, notes scribbled on my arms like a cheat sheet, coffee going cold next to the console. It's like time knew I was leaving and had decided to speed up out of spite.

People kept poking their heads in—some with questions, others with weird half-smiles, like they didn't know if they were supposed to congratulate me or pretend it was just another Monday. I kept it light. Laughed. Said things like, "Still here for another thirteen days, don't write me off yet." But inside, I was already starting to detach. It wasn't bitterness. It was more like my roots were pulling up from the soil, getting ready to be planted somewhere else.

By late afternoon, the studio was quieter. I plugged in my headphones and finished mixing a piece I'd been holding onto for a while—a personal one. It wouldn't air. It was more of a time capsule, my voice layered over years of late nights and too-loud headphones and deadlines no one else understood. A quiet goodbye.

I still had a hundred things to finish before I clocked out, and my inbox was already judging me. But for a moment, I just sat there. Let the silence settle. Two weeks. That's all I had left in this booth, in this version of me. I planned to make every second count.

After hammering through most of the piles of work on my desk, I finally made it home. Even though I was tired beyond belief, I mustered up enough strength to throw together a small dinner for me and Jermaine, so we could hopefully talk, come to a final understanding, and maybe get the details on the conversations between him and Rhonda.

At seven o'clock, a knock at my door interrupted me as I finished up the spaghetti and was taking the bread out of the oven.

"Better late than never, I suppose," I teased, opening the door and glancing at the wall clock that read 7:01.

"My bad. Had to make a stop at the liquor store to grab some wine."

"No problem," I said. "Come on in."

Jermaine stepped inside and headed straight for the kitchen.

"Whatever you're cooking smells good. Damn, it's hard to find a woman who knows her way around the kitchen," he said playfully.

"Thank you. It's just a little spaghetti and garlic bread. It's a recipe I got from my grandmother. The sauce is homemade. She used to make her sauce with crushed tomatoes but I use fire roasted and I think it makes the sauce a bit more tangy, *and* you have to stir it just right."

"Well, I will have to thank your grandmother when I see her. It smells amazing in here," Jermaine said, grabbing a plate from the top shelf of the cabinet.

"Here," I said, taking the plate from his hand. "Let me fix your food. Have a seat at the table."

He flashed that beautiful smile that I'd grown to both love and hate. It's funny how the line between those two emotions can blur when you're going through a lot with someone. I began to fix his plate by placing a medium slice of garlic bread on his plate, followed by a heaping mound of spaghetti topped with my grandmother's meat sauce. I put the plate in front of him and headed back to the kitchen to fix my own. I placed the bottle of wine on the table and Jermaine poured us both a glass. He took a big fork full of spaghetti and a sip of his wine.

"So, I hear you're headed to Townsend as the PD. Congrats," he said casually while continuing to eat his food.

"Thank you. It's definitely time for a change," I said, sipping my wine and taking a seat at the dinner table.

"Yeah, that's what I keep telling you."

"Oh . . . hey," I exclaimed, glancing over the table at the feast I'd prepared. "I forgot the butter for the garlic bread. Let me grab it from the fridge."

As I got up to make my way to the kitchen, Jermaine gently grabbed my arm and pulled me close to him so I was sitting on his lap. Gazing into my eyes, he moved in and began to kiss me deeply, moaning and caressing my back.

I barely had a chance to react before his hands were all over me, his lips trailing down my neck to my breasts. He wasn't wasting time. He lifted me onto the kitchen counter, his gaze dark with intent.

"I've got you tonight," he murmured.

He pushed me down, hiked up my skirt, and tore my panties with his teeth. His tongue worked me until I came on his fingers. Then, without hesitation, he carried me to the bedroom and finished what he had started.

Lying beside him afterward, I glanced over. He was staring at me with an unreadable expression.

"Why are you looking at me like that?" I asked.

"Because I think you deserve better than what you're getting."

I groaned. "Oh God, I don't want to get into the Kevin stuff with you tonight. Can we just enjoy this moment?"

"We could have moments like this all the time," he said. "I'm not trying to be a cock blocker, but Kevin is foul. Have you ever cheated on him? I mean, other than with me?"

His question dragged me back to my college days—when Alicia and I were both pregnant, and Kevin promised he'd be with me if I took care of the situation.

"Ann," Jermaine said, snapping me back to the present. "Did you hear me?"

"Uh, yeah, I heard you," I replied. "Kevin and I have been through a lot since college. I always thought we could get through anything. But lately, I've been thinking I need to leave him. It's just . . . I've never seen him cheat with my own eyes."

"What do you mean? Didn't you catch him at Rhonda's house?"

"Yeah, but she was just helping him with his resume. I didn't actually see them together."

"Wow, that dude's got you brainwashed. I'm telling you, they're both foul. You can do so much better."

"Jermaine, you don't understand. I'm not leaving him. Kevin and I are in love. We've both done things we regret, and we're trying to work them out. I don't need you reminding me every day that I should leave him and that you're better for me. I'm really sick of it!"

"You're the most delusional person I've ever met. Fine, stay with him," Jermaine said, getting dressed abruptly. "You always talk about loyalty," he yelled from the living room, "but where was your loyalty just a few minutes ago?"

I got up, slipped into my bathrobe, and found Jermaine putting on his shoes in the living room.

"Are you leaving?"

"Yeah, I think I need to go."

I sat down next to him on the couch. "Don't leave. I'm so lost right now. All I do is cry. I can't focus on work, and I don't have an appetite. Jermaine, it's just so hard."

Tears began to fall. Jermaine pulled me close and caressed me gently. I couldn't believe he was comforting me, especially given everything.

"It's okay, baby. I've got you."

"Jermaine, I know I need to leave Kevin, but it's so hard. We've been through so much . . ."

"Yeah, you've been through a lot. But sometimes you need to let the past go and move on. Stop holding on to what you think you had." Jermaine was right. "So, when are you gonna tell him?" he asked.

"Tell him what?" I asked, startled.

"Tell him about us."

"Wait, wait, wait. I didn't say anything about telling Kevin yet."

"Ann, you know I want you, and I know you want me. We could be good together. Let's make this happen." He stroked my cheek, eyes locked earnestly on mine.

"I'm not sure I want to tell him anything about us. If I leave Kevin, it'll be because our relationship isn't working, not because I want to be with someone else. I can't just jump from one relationship into another."

Jermaine was clearly frustrated. He stood up, looking at me with an intensity I'd never seen before. I grabbed his arm, hoping to prevent him from leaving.

"You're really good at playing the victim, like someone did something to you. I know I'm not the first person you've slept with while you were in this supposed relationship with Kevin."

"What are you talking about?"

"You heard me. Always talking about loyalty but sneaking around. Answer me this: am I the only person you've cheated on Kevin with?"

I thought about Cory. I couldn't tell Jermaine about that night in Atlanta. I didn't want to seem like a whore. Kevin and I had been going through so much then, and I didn't want to leave him. I'd never faced our issues directly, so I sought comfort elsewhere.

"You not gonna answer me?"

"Answer what?" I said, irritated.

"Am I the only person you've ever cheated on Kevin with?"

"YES! YES! I would never have done this if I wasn't unsure about my relationship with Kevin."

"Then you need to tell him it's over. I'm not going to be the second choice, and if you don't tell him, I will."

Jermaine pulled away from me and stormed out, slamming the door behind him. I realized I had created a mess. Using Jermaine to cope with the issues between me and Kevin was turning out to be a terrible idea. Now I faced the possibility of Jermaine revealing everything to Kevin. Given their previous encounter, Kevin might believe what Jermaine said. I needed to keep Jermaine away, but how? I had hoped that the new job at Townsend would help me leave the drama behind, but it seemed like it would follow me wherever I went.

CHAPTER 15

UNRAVELING THREADS

It was a Saturday morning, one of those rare, crisp days when the city felt alive in a way that was different from the usual hustle. I was at the station—not for work, but to clear out my office. Two weeks had passed since I handed in my resignation, and now it was time to sever the final tie. Townsend Communications was waiting for me on Monday. I had briefly considered taking some time off to give myself a chance to breathe before diving into a new role. But the thought of staying home, stewing over the wreckage of my personal life. It like a mental prison sentence I wasn't ready to serve.

I had asked Keith and the rest of the team to skip the whole farewell party ritual. It was the last thing I wanted—a staged gathering of small talk and forced smiles. I just wanted to pack up and leave, slipping quietly into the next chapter, closing this one with no more fanfare than the final click of a door latch.

The past two weeks had been a minefield, especially with Jermaine walking the halls, that smug smile never leaving his face. After that night at my apartment, I had expected coldness, anger, maybe even a bitter confrontation. Yet, he was unfailingly polite, almost too cordial, which somehow made it worse. And he never mentioned what had happened, not even in passing. So, naturally, I didn't bring it up either. We floated through those last days in a strange, unspoken truce.

I packed the last box and carried it to my car, the weight not just from my things but from the finality of it all. After closing the trunk, I took the envelope with my office keys and slid it under Keith's door, adding a short note: "See you when the rankings drop." I signed it with a smiley face, though my heart wasn't in it. Then, I walked out of the station one last time, drove home, and tried not to think too much about what I was leaving behind.

Monday arrived, bringing with it a new beginning. As I stepped into the sleek lobby of Townsend Communications, nerves fluttered in my stomach. Before I could introduce myself to the receptionist, she greeted me with a warm smile.

"Good morning, Ms. Parkens. How are you today?"

Her voice was bright, almost musical. "Mr. Townsend and the team are waiting for you in the conference room. Please, go right in."

She gestured toward an elegant set of double doors.

"Uh . . . Good morning," I stammered, momentarily thrown by how prepared she was.

"I'm sorry, your name is . . . ?"

"Tammie."

"Nice to meet you, Tammie." I extended my hand, noting how young and eager she appeared.

"You too. We're glad to have another woman around here," she said, shaking my hand with a friendly firmness.

"Thank you," I managed to say, feeling a faint warmth from her words. With a final nod, I turned toward the double doors, steeling myself for what lay beyond.

I took a deep breath and pushed the door open. Inside, the room was filled with people seated around a massive mahogany conference table, polished to a gleam. Mr. Townsend and Mr. Hamilton stood near the front, looking expectant.

"Well, there she is, our new fearless leader," Mr. Townsend announced with a wide smile, striding toward me.

"Everyone, this is your new program director, Angela Parkens. We finally stole her from across the street. So yes, she has made the switch!"

Polite applause filled the room as I followed him to the front, feeling the weight of all those eyes on me.

"Mr. Hamilton, how are you?" I greeted, extending my hand.

"Enough with the formalities, Ann. We've got you now," he replied, gripping my hand firmly. "Please, call me Richard."

"Okay . . . Richard." I smiled, trying to ease the tightness in my chest.

"Ann," Mr. Townsend began, his voice warm but firm. "Derrick couldn't be here; he left for Orlando early. He's offered his help if you need anything, just a phone call away."

"Okay, thanks."

"Alright, team," Mr. Townsend clapped his hands together. "Let's go around and introduce ourselves."

I sat down and listened as each person gave their introduction, their names tumbling around in my head like pieces of a puzzle. I knew I wouldn't remember them all; names never stuck unless I worked closely with someone. But I nodded and smiled, doing my best to convey warmth and openness.

When it was my turn, I stood, clearing my throat.

"I'm so glad to be here, and I look forward to working with all of you. I know it can be unnerving when a new program director comes in, but let me ease your minds—I'm not here to make sweeping changes. We're here to improve our sound and our presence in the community. This is a team effort, and I believe we have what it takes to become the number one station in this market."

Applause filled the room again, a bit more genuine this time. I could feel some of the tension ease.

"Alright, folks, now that we've all met, let's get back to work," Mr. Townsend said, dismissing the group. He turned to me with a smile.

"Come on, Ann. Let me show you to your office." As we walked through the building, passing the break room and rounding a corner to another set of double doors, I felt a flutter of anticipation.

"Are you ready? We fixed it up just for you," he said with a flourish. He swung the doors open, and my jaw dropped.

The office was enormous, nearly the size of my entire apartment. A gleaming mahogany desk stood at its center, paired with a grand credenza and bookshelves that lined the walls. A conference table with four rolling chairs sat in one corner, while a 36-inch television, complete with cable, hung elegantly on the opposite wall.

"Is this to your liking?" Mr. Townsend asked, his eyes twinkling.

"Yes, this is perfect," I replied, unable to stop the smile spreading across my face. It was more than perfect; it felt like validation.

"Well, I figured you'd be delegating most of your production duties now that you're leaving those behind at the other station," he said with a laugh. I laughed too, more out of relief than anything.

"Well, I might want to polish up my skills . . . you know."

"Yeah, I get that." He nodded. "Alright, I'll give you some time to settle in. We'll meet Richard for lunch later, okay?"

"Sounds good."

As he left, he closed the double doors. moving to sit behind the massive desk. I leaned back in the chair, the leather creaking softly, and exhaled. *I've finally arrived,* I thought. The months ahead would be grueling, but they'd be mine. I had worked hard to get here, and now, I had my own space, my own team.

Over the next several months, with work demanding my focus, my personal life naturally fell to the wayside. It wasn't a conscious decision; it was more of a survival mechanism. I had to step away from the chaos that had been my love life.

Jermaine's threat to tell Kevin about our past still lingered like a dark cloud, but changing jobs gave me a convenient way to avoid him. I changed both my phone numbers, landline and cell, to dodge his calls—especially the ones that might come when Kevin was around. I wasn't ready to let Kevin go, despite the growing chasm between us. Yet, even with Jermaine "under control," Kevin and I continued to drift apart. We spent less and less time together, and the intimacy we once shared was nonexistent.

The success of my new role meant more late nights promoting our station and rekindling connections with club owners I had worked with before. But now, Kevin wouldn't accompany me, not even when I asked. His absence was yet another silent brick in the wall that had sprung up between us. I tried everything: dinners, candlelit nights, soft music, wine. But every time, Kevin would simply shower and head to bed, ignoring my attempts. Other times, he wouldn't come home at all, calling later to say he'd be staying at his parents' house. Eventually, I grew numb to his indifference, and the fire to fix what was broken died. It didn't seem to bother him either. He didn't even acknowledge how drastically things had changed between us. Six months passed, each one colder than the last. Kevin spent more nights away, and I found myself sinking deeper into my work, using it as a shield from the harsh reality of my crumbling relationship.

One afternoon, I left the office early and decided to call him, hoping maybe we could meet for dinner. When I rang the detention center where he worked, the officer on duty informed me that Kevin hadn't shown up that day. I hung up and sat there, staring blankly at the wall. My mind buzzed with questions, but I shut them down. I wasn't ready to face whatever truths lay beneath his absence. Instead, I picked up the phone and dialed a different number.

"Hello?"

The voice was familiar, a steadying force for my reeling mind.

"Hey, Jermaine. It's Ann."

"Well, well, well," he replied, a hint of amusement in his tone. "You become a program director and change your number. What's up with that?"

"I needed some time," I said flatly. "Look, I didn't call for that. I want to see you."

"You do?" He sounded genuinely surprised.

"Yes. Can you come over when you get off? No sex. I just want to talk, okay?"

There was a pause, then, "Okay. I'll be there at six."

"See you then."

I hung up, feeling both relief and dread. Six o'clock came, and when the doorbell rang, I felt my heartbeat quicken. I let him in, and we sat down, the air thick with tension.

We talked about everything—the stations, our careers, the transformations we had each seen in the past six months. He told me how proud he was of what I had accomplished, and for a moment, I felt seen in a way I hadn't for so long.

"You still look good to me," he said, his eyes holding mine in a way that made my pulse quicken.

"Thanks," I replied, forcing a smile. I needed this, even if I didn't fully understand why.

"So, has Keith been treating you well?" I asked.

"Yeah, he's cool," Jermaine said, but then he shifted, his gaze growing more serious. "But listen, I'm tired of talking about work.

How have you been? I know we didn't leave things on a good note, and despite everything, I do care about what happens to you."

"I know," I whispered, the words tasting like truth.

"You know, I spoke to your girl," he added, his tone changing.

"Rhonda?" I asked, my stomach tightening.

"Yeah. She told me she helped your boy get his resume together."

My heart skipped a beat.

The words hit me like a barrage of arrows, each one embedding itself in my mind without an end in sight.

"Ann?" Jermaine's voice sliced through the fog of my thoughts, sharp and probing. "You okay?" His eyes narrowed slightly, searching my face as if trying to read my mind.

"Oh, yeah, I'm good." I forced a smile, a brittle thing that barely held itself together. My heart pounded in my chest, each beat echoing through the stillness of the room.

I had to keep my composure. I had to stay in control. This was not the time to unravel—not in front of Jermaine, not again. Not when I was barely holding onto the pieces of my own sanity.

CHAPTER 16

LOVE AND RADIO

When I walked into work that morning, I knew I had to keep my head clear. The morning started out like any other until I received a call from Kevin's father, Mr. Bostick. I hadn't heard from him in months. He had called me a few hours earlier, casually asking about the state of my relationship with his son. I had been eaten up by guilt the entire time as I lied, telling him everything was fine. I was unnerved by the tone of his voice during the call. It sounded as though he had something else to tell me but I didn't have time to have such a deep conversation so early in the morning.

The conversation stuck in my mind throughout the morning though, and I tried to brush it off. The promotions meeting with the new restaurant was today, and the station's account executive was hell-bent on landing this client. He'd been trying for weeks to convince them to advertise with us. I adjusted my jacket, straightened my shoulders, and stepped through the doorway.

Tammie intercepted me almost immediately, holding a note in her hand, her eyes wide with urgency.

"Hey, Ann," she said, pressing the paper into my palm. "Your mother called. She wants you to call her back as soon as possible."

"My mother?" I echoed, caught off guard. It felt like a punch to the gut. I hadn't spoken to her in years. Apparently, it was going to be that kind of day. A day of reunions. Phone calls from everyone who I hadn't spoken to in a very long stretch of time. My mother, though, was a bit more evasive than Mr. Bostick. I was used to *her* being halfway across the world in Europe, neck-deep in international business, too busy to spare a thought for family.

I barely knew her growing up; she'd left me with my grandmother and treated our relationship more like a business arrangement. So, if she was calling now, it could only mean one thing: she had some scheme in the works that would make her more money.

Trying to suppress the rush of emotions, I walked briskly down the hall to my office. My mind was already racing as I dialed her international number. To my surprise, she picked up on the first ring.

"Baaaaby," she said warmly. "I'm so glad you got back to me. And so promptly, I might add. I see your business acumen is improving. There is nothing like a prompt response to throw your prospect off their game. That's a good trait to have in acquisitions. Doesn't give them time to react."

My mom. Always finding a way to bring business into a conversation. Even with a daughter she hadn't spoken to in years. Not the normal conversation you would expect between a mother and a daughter but then again, nothing about our relationship was normal.

"Hey, Mom," I said, struggling to sound casual. "Good to hear your voice."

"It's so good to talk to you too, honey," she replied smoothly. Her voice had that familiar crispness, like champagne bubbling over polished steel. "How have you been?"

"Good," I lied through my teeth. I wasn't about to tell her about the mess with Kevin. She never liked him anyway, and I wasn't about to give her more ammunition.

"Listen," she continued, her tone sharpening. "I know this is an expensive call, so I'll get straight to the point. You know I'm all about business and I have my ear to the ground in all aspects, *especially* when it comes to my baby girl."

"Yes, Mom. I know you have contacts everywhere so whatever moves I make, I know they have to be strategic. I wouldn't want to tarnish the Parkens name in the business world," I said, trying not to sound too sarcastic but hoping she would pick up on my attitude.

"Yes, darling, of course," she said, not acknowledging my tone at all. "Anyway," she pushed onward. I could hear her eyes roll through the phone. "I hear you're turning Townsend into a cash cow."

I blinked in surprise.

"You heard that all the way from Europe?"

"Baby, you just said it yourself, you know I have eyes and ears everywhere. I know everything about business," she chuckled. And she wasn't lying.

"So listen up, I have a conference call with a group of shareholders in ten," she continued. "I had a chat with my old friend Frank, and guess what?"

"What?" I asked, bracing myself.

"He wants to sell."

"Sell? What do you mean sell? Sell Townsend Communications?" My heart skipped a beat.

"Yep."

"Damn," I muttered, rubbing my temple. "I just got here. Are you giving me a heads up that I need to start looking for another job?"

She laughed, a sound as smooth as silk. "Quite the contrary, baby. He's selling to me. He's meeting with my lawyer and finance people to hammer out the details as we speak, and hopefully, we will have the deal finalized before close of business today. I really want this to be done quickly because I have other matters to attend to, but you know how slow men are. They can't make up their minds unless you nudge them a bit. At any rate, once this deal goes through, I need the strongest possible team in place to handle the day to day and you know I can't run a radio station from over here, so I'm signing it over to you. Isn't that fantastic news?"

I could almost hear the smile in her voice, thick with satisfaction. My breath caught in my throat.

"Mom, oh my God! You mean . . . ?"

"Yep, baby. When this deal is done, Townsend will be yours."

I shot up from my chair, letting out a scream that startled Tammie down the hall. This was unreal. My mother—this elusive business tycoon—was actually buying a radio station and handing it over to me. For once, I didn't wish for her to be a regular soccer mom with a station wagon, attending PTA meetings.

This . . . this was something else entirely.

"Ann, are you okay, baby?" she asked, amusement lacing her voice.

"Yeah, Mom, I'm fine," I managed, swallowing the lump in my throat.

"I know this is sudden. But this has been in the works ever since you took that job with Frank. We've been maneuvering you into his stations for a while now."

"So, this was part of your plan all along?" I asked, a mix of awe and resentment coloring my voice.

"Of course. I want my baby to be successful." A brief pause, and then her voice shifted back to business. "Anyway, I have to jump on this shareholder's call. Frank will meet with you today to go over everything, alright?"

"Okay, Mom. Thank you so much. I love you." The words escaped easily from my mouth.

"Love you too, baby."

I hung up, staring at the phone in my hand. Townsend would be mine. The words echoed in my mind, a surreal mantra I couldn't fully grasp.

That evening, as soon as I got home, I rushed to the phone to call Kevin. No answer at the detention center. Fine, I'd try his parents' house since his dad called me this morning. Maybe they'd know where he was.

Mr. Bostick answered on the second ring.

"Hello?" His voice was gruff, as if he'd just woken up.

"Hello, Mr. Bostick. This is Ann," I said, trying to keep my voice steady.

"Well . . . hello, Ann. Twice in one day I get to hear your lovely voice." He sounded surprised, almost wary.

"Yes, sir. Um, I was wondering, is Kevin there? Could I speak with him, please?"

"Kevin?" A pause. "He hasn't been here in weeks. I think he's out of town. He won't be back until next week. Didn't he tell you about the trip?"

"What?" My stomach dropped. "Oooh . . . you know what, he did," I lied, my face flushing. "It must've slipped my mind. So much going on at work; I just forgot. Thanks, though. It was good talking to you, again."

"You too. And hey . . . don't be a stranger. Come see us sometime. You don't need Kevin to bring you over. You know how to get here."

"I will, sir. Take care," I replied, forcing a smile through the phone.

I hung up, my legs giving way as I sank to the floor. Tears welled up, spilling in hot, silent streams. I curled into a ball, sobbing until exhaustion took me under and I fell asleep on the floor.

The phone's ring startled me awake. I glanced at the clock—11:30 p.m. Five hours had passed. Groggy and disoriented, I grabbed the phone.

"Hello?" I croaked, my voice raspy.

"Hey, Ann," Jermaine's voice came through, tense and unsettled.

"Jermaine?" I blinked, sitting up. "What's up?"

"Yeah, you busy?" His voice was sharper than usual.

"Just waking up. Look, I can't really talk right now—"

"This'll only take a sec," he interrupted. "You know all those talks we've had about you and Kevin, right?"

"Yeah, what about them?" I snapped, irritation flaring up inside me.

"Well, sometimes I feel like you're just using me to get over him," he said, his words cutting deep. "I mean, you don't have any genuine feelings for me, do you?"

I sighed, brushing my disheveled hair back. "Do we have to do this now? You know how I feel about you. And you know how I feel about Kevin. We've been through this before. Whatever feelings I have for you aren't enough to make me leave him."

"So, you are using me?" he pressed, his tone cold and relentless.

Silence stretched between us before he asked, "Am I the only person you've ever cheated on Kevin with?"

My heart skipped a beat. My jaw clenched.

"You've asked me that before, and I'm tired of this conversation," I said coolly. He wasn't getting anything about Cory out of me. Not now. Not ever.

"Well, answer me again," Jermaine pushed, his voice like ice.

A surge of anger boiled inside me. "YES, DAMN IT!" I shouted, my voice trembling with rage and regret. "You are the only person I cheated with!"

Silence.

And then, like a bomb detonating, a voice cut through the line.

"ANN!"

My blood ran cold. It was Kevin.

Jermaine's laughter sliced through the moment, sharp and cruel.

"I knew this shit was going to catch up with you," Kevin snarled.

The ground beneath me collapsed, leaving me in free fall—a mess of regret, anger, and helplessness.

A sharp knock on the door jolts me out of my daze. I blink hard, the fog of the last memory dissipating like mist in the morning sun. My office snaps back into focus—the sleek mahogany desk, the faint hum of the city outside. I glance down, realizing I am clutching the phone on my table, gripping it like a lifeline to a past I thought I'd buried.

"Ms. Parkens?" Tanya's voice drifts into the room, soft yet firm. She steps in cautiously as though sensing the storm brewing beneath my calm façade. Her presence is grounding and intrusive, dragging me back to the present with an unsettling abruptness.

"It's getting late. Do you still need me?"

I glance at the clock on the wall and force myself to breathe, the air feeling heavy as it fills my lungs. I should be heading out.

"It's fine," I sigh, managing a smile. "Have a lovely evening, Tanya!"

The whirlwind of emotions, vivid and raw, reluctantly settles into a dull ache in the pit of my stomach.

How many years have passed since that chaotic chapter with Kevin and Jermaine? It feels like another lifetime, yet its ghosts still haunt me, lurking in the corners of my mind. My office, with its polished wood and carefully curated elegance, seems like a universe away from the mess I once clawed my way out of. The symbols of success—the framed accolades on the wall, the sweeping city view—none of it hints at the wreckage I'd left behind to stand here.

That drama and those reckless decisions have scarred me in ways I am still discovering. It made me wary, cautious of women like Rhonda, whose smiles now feel like knives. And it made me incapable of letting any man close enough to hurt me again.

It forged this version of me: a thirty-six-year-old radio station owner, single, guarded, and far too acquainted with loneliness. And now, here I am, after firing half of my on-air staff because of our plummeting ratings. I can't help but feel a bitter twist of irony.

My mother bought this station for me, charting out a future I had never fully chosen. But life had other plans, and so did she.

Straightening my blazer, I push back my hair, forcing composure as I reach for my bag. My hand hovers over the cool metal handle of the double doors. I hesitate, allowing myself one fleeting glance around my office. It isn't just a workspace; it is proof of everything I've endured, every sacrifice that has carved out the person I have become.

Could it really be mine, this life I am leading? Is this the success I had dreamt of, or is it just another role I am playing to survive?

With a deep breath, I grip the handle and open the doors, stepping out into the hallway. My heels click against the polished hardwood floor, each step reminding me of the path I had chosen. There is no going back now, no undoing the years, the decisions, the scars. There is only forward.

OFF THE AIR

I make my way to the parking garage, each step echoing with the weight of the day. The oppressive exhaustion clings to me like a heavy cloak. I reach my car, unlock the door, and sink into the driver's seat, feeling the mental strain of the day settle deep into my bones. I need something—anything—to clear my mind. Before I start the engine, I pull out my phone and dial Brianna's number.

The cacophony of music, laughter, and clinking glasses greets me.

"Hey, girl, where are you?" Brianna's voice bursts through the phone, vibrant and unrestrained. "We're living it up without you, Ann!"

"Hey, girl," I respond, trying to match her energy. "I'm just leaving the office, heading that way. Go ahead and order my drink. You know what I want."

"Okay, I got you!" Her excitement is contagious.

"Hold on. Also, order some of those Italian herb cheese sticks. I need something to soak up the alcohol."

"Aiight. See you in a bit." The line goes dead.

Twenty minutes later, I pull up to the lounge to meet my girls and hand my keys to the valet. Stepping out of the car, the cool night air feels like a welcome embrace. I'm looking forward to this night—not just to drown out the day's turmoil with cocktails but because it's been far too long since we've all gathered.

We are a group of accomplished women, our careers demanding more of us than we often give ourselves credit for. Yet, it's this very dedication that has fueled our success.

Brianna, a college friend, now runs her makeup line tailored for those with acne and skin issues. She's carved out a niche market, creating a brand that speaks to those often overlooked.

Manika, whom I met through Brianna, is a serial wife turned entrepreneur. Instead of living off her alimony, she invested her wealth into a luxury handbag line, which skyrocketed after one of her bags appeared on a popular reality show.

My friends—they're more than friends. They're my sisters. We've weathered life's storms together, and tonight, I'm deeply grateful for the bond that's kept us close.

As I enter the lounge, I spot them at a table near the dance floor, surrounded by three striking men. Their presence seems to have transformed the empty chairs of a nearby table into a lively gathering. I make my way over, and Brianna looks up with a broad, somewhat tipsy smile.

"Hey, Ann!" she exclaims, her voice bubbling with excitement. Manika chimes in with their enthusiastic greetings.

When I reach the table, we embrace warmly, and one of the men pulls out a chair for me.

"Bryson, this is my good friend, Ann. Ann, meet Bryson," Brianna introduces us.

Bryson flashes me a dazzling smile.

"Nice to meet you, Ann."

"Nice to meet you too," I reply, settling into the chair. Brianna continues.

"And these are his friends: Michael and Juane." Bryson points to each guy.

"Hello," I say, offering a genuine smile. "Nice to meet everyone."

"Here's your drink, Ann," Brianna says, sliding a glass my way.

"You need to catch up!" Manika says, her hand comforting on my shoulder, then adds, "Brianna told us about the station. I'm so sorry about everything. You know we're here for you if you need anything."

"Thank you, ladies," I say, touched by their concern. "I love you all for being here, but let's not dwell on that. We're here to enjoy the night, so let's do just that."

"Sounds good to me," Bryson says, clinking his glass against mine.

Even though my intention is to unwind with my friends and not to meet anyone new, the men's engaging conversation throughout the night is a pleasant surprise. They might as well have stepped off the cover of a men's magazine, each holding more charm than the last.

The night unfolds with us drinking, laughing, and dancing. The pulsating rhythm of the music and the vibrant ambiance start to lift the heavy veil of stress that clung to me all day.

In this moment, surrounded by laughter and the warmth of my friends, I momentarily forget the chaos of tomorrow. My focus is on being present, savoring the companionship of these extraordinary women who have stood by me through thick and thin.

We're dressed to the nines, and our laughter fills the room. As the evening progresses, conversations flow freely, mingling shared memories with future dreams. With each sip, the weight of responsibility melts away, replaced by a rare sense of liberation and joy.

We dance with abandon, celebrating the freedom and pleasure of being alive. Hours slip by unnoticed until I glance at my watch. It's fifteen minutes past midnight. Regretfully, I know it's time to end the night.

"Ann," Brianna says, noticing my glance. "I know you're about to head out. I'm not even gonna argue with you this time."

Usually, I'm the one who leaves early, and Brianna tries to convince me to stay. Tonight, though, she understands why I need to go.

"I'm really sorry to cut it short," I say, standing up. "I've got a big day tomorrow, and I've already stayed longer than planned."

We exchange hugs and the usual "get home safe" and "call us when you get home" farewells. As I reach for my purse, Bryson gently grabs my wrist.

"Ann, I get that you have to leave, but I wanted to say I really enjoyed tonight. I was hoping we could see each other again."

For a moment, I contemplate his offer. The ease of our conversation was refreshing, and he seems genuinely nice. But the reality is that I can't take on anything new right now. I'm not ready to dive into another relationship, to learn about someone else's life, or to accommodate another person's needs. I just want to focus on myself and the life I'm building. I smile and pull him aside for a more private moment.

"Bryson, I've really enjoyed tonight . . ."

"But," he interrupts, sensing what's coming.

I laugh softly.

"Yes, but I've got a lot going on right now. It's just not the right time for me. I hope you can understand."

He smiles, offering a warm hug. "I understand. Thanks for a great evening. Get home safe."

I wave to my friends one last time and head toward the door. Stepping out into the cool night air, I feel a lightness in my heart. The memories of tonight will linger long after the music fades and the lights dim.

As the valet brings my car around, I realize that despite life's imperfections, I'm extraordinarily lucky to have these remarkable women and the strength to keep moving forward.

Sliding into the driver's seat, I take a deep breath of the crisp night air. I'm heading home, knowing exactly what awaits me when I arrive. A huge California King-sized bed, with reports, folders, and a laptop on one side and me on the other. But I know this life—messy, beautiful, and full of potential—is mine. And right now, that's more than enough.

THE END

EPILOGUE

The evening air buzzed with anticipation as the grand opening of The Capital Grille, CCI's latest culinary venture, drew a lively crowd. The restaurant hummed with energy—clinking glasses, laughter, and the tantalizing aromas wafting from the kitchen. At a table draped in crisp white linen sat James Chestly, settled in, his mind racing with thoughts of the future as he engaged in deep conversation with other CCI executives.

Tonight's dinner held significance, not just for the restaurant, but for a potential partnership that could transform the media landscape.

He glanced toward the entrance just as I walked through the door. I had chosen a chic yet understated outfit that I felt radiated both confidence and warmth. As I approached, James stood and offered a genuine smile.

"Angela, it's great to see you again," he said, extending his hand. "I'm so glad you accepted my invitation."

"James, it's wonderful to see you again as well," I replied, my grip firm yet friendly.

We quickly fell into a lively conversation with other station owners and James's counterparts at CCI, the air thick with the anticipation of possibilities. I'm not sure why I felt so secure in this mixed company. Still, before long, I was sharing stories of my station—its challenges in competing with larger media entities and my unwavering commitment to serving the community.

James and his counterparts listened intently, drawn in by my passion and resilience.

We sat down for dinner, and as the first course arrived—a beautifully plated, adventurous dish—the conversation took a turn toward ideas for collaboration in the future. James had a brilliant vision for integrating media platforms, and I couldn't help but appreciate his focus on authenticity in storytelling. With my connections to the local culture and community, I was sure I could help push those stories to new audiences and create something wonderful together.

With each subsequent course, we connected even more. The conversation flowed effortlessly, laughter punctuating our discussions as the wine poured freely.

By the time dessert arrived—a decadent tiramisu—we were no longer just two industry players meeting for dinner. We were collaborators, each excited by the potential of what we could create together.

I leaned back, a thoughtful expression crossing my face.

"I imagine a series where we highlight local stories—voices that don't always get the spotlight they deserve," I stated.

James nodded, his eyes lighting up. "Absolutely. Let's make it a celebration of community and creativity."

As we clinked glasses, sealing our newfound partnership, the atmosphere around us crackled with energy. The night was more than a meal; it marked the beginning of a journey that could reshape our industries, blending my grassroots authenticity with James's expansive vision.

After a wonderful dinner and delightful conversation, I glanced at my watch and realized it was time to call it a night. I thanked James for such a memorable evening, and he escorted me toward the main entrance. As we stepped out into the bustling night, the city felt alive with possibility. James leaned forward, seriousness and playfulness dancing across his face.

"I think it's because we share a vision. You're not just a radio station owner. You're a storyteller, and so am I. We complement each other."

I felt my heart flutter. Could there be something more profound developing between James and me? A connection that went beyond work? The spark was undeniable, and we locked eyes. At that moment, I sensed we were on the cusp of something new.

"Where do we go from here?" I asked, my voice soft but steady.

"Wherever we want," James replied, a grin spreading across his face. "We could keep pushing boundaries in media . . . or . . ." He paused, his grin sly and playful. "We could explore this . . . whatever this is between us. I'd love to see where it leads."

My heart raced. I had built a successful career from the ground up, and now, with James by my side as a business partner, maybe he could finally tear down the walls I had built around my heart. The future was full of possibilities, and I was ready to embrace them—both personally and professionally.

As I left the restaurant, for the first time in a long time, I felt like I could finally breathe. With James, I felt inspired, adventurous, and deeply connected. Whatever lay ahead, I knew we would face it together, a powerful duo ready to make our mark on the world. Together!

LET'S TALK ABOUT IT

Whether you're reading *Love and Radio* on your own or diving in with a book club, the following discussion questions are designed to help you explore the deeper themes, choices, and emotions within the story. These prompts aim to spark meaningful conversations and personal reflection as you think about Ann's journey—and maybe even your own.

Take your time, reflect honestly, and don't be afraid to sit with the questions that challenge you most. After all, the most powerful stories are the ones that inspire us to look inward, ask big questions, and grow.

Reader Discussion Questions + Self-Reflective Prompts

1. **Ann struggles to balance personal ambition and emotional vulnerability.** *In what ways do her past and her career influence her decisions in love and life?*

Reflect: Have you ever faced a moment where your ambition clashed with your emotional needs? How did you handle it?

2. **The relationship between Ann and her mother is layered and complex.** *How does their dynamic shape the story? What role does forgiveness play in their journey?*

Reflect: Is there someone in your life whom you've had to forgive in order to move forward? What did that process look like for you?

3. **Friendship is a strong theme throughout the book.** *How do Ann's friendships help her cope with professional and personal challenges? Do you think they empowered or distracted her at times?*

Reflect: Do your friendships support your growth, or do they ever hold you back? How do you tell the difference?

4. ***Love and Radio* explores the difficulty of letting go of the past.** *How do Ann's experiences with Kevin influence her view of new relationships?*

Reflect: Are there past experiences or relationships that still shape how you approach love today?

5. **Bryson seems like a promising romantic prospect.** *Why do you think Ann ultimately turns him down? Did you agree with her decision?*

Reflect: Have you ever had to say no to something good because it wasn't right for you at the time?

6. **The radio station becomes a symbol of legacy and identity.** *What does taking over the station represent for Ann? How does this affect her view of success?*

Reflect: What does success look like for you? How much of that definition is shaped by your personal story or legacy?

7. **The novel blends ambition, heartbreak, and healing.** *Which theme resonated with you most and why?*

Reflect: What season of life are you currently in—pursuing, recovering, or rebuilding?

8. **What did you think of the ending?** *Were you satisfied with where Ann landed in her personal and professional life?*

Reflect: If your story were a book, where would this current chapter end?

9. **How did Dee Dee Redding's background in radio influence the realism of the story?** *Did you feel immersed in that world?*

Reflect: Have you ever worked in a space or industry that shaped your identity or outlook?

10. **If you could ask Ann one question, what would it be?**

 Reflect: If someone asked *you* that same question, what would your honest answer be?

ACKNOWLEDGEMENTS

This book would not have been possible without the support and encouragement of many remarkable individuals. First and foremost, I am deeply grateful to my son for his unwavering love and belief in me, even during the moments when I doubted myself. Your patience and understanding have been the foundation upon which this project was built. Second, I would like to thank my fur babies, Rocko and Maya, for sitting at my feet for hours while I typed away at the computer. Also, a huge thank you to my girlfriends for being my sounding boards, for your understanding, and for your constant reminder that this journey was worth every step—15 years in the making. Last but certainly not least, I would like to thank K and R for the material. Without your betrayal, I wouldn't have had anything to write about.

ABOUT THE AUTHOR

Dee Dee Redding is a first-time novelist with a passion for storytelling that blends rich character development with captivating worlds. Born in Atlanta, GA and raised in rural Jones County, GA, Dee Dee has always been fascinated by the power of fiction to transport readers to new realms and perspectives. She holds a degree in broadcast journalism from GA College and State University in Milledgeville, GA and spent over 20 years of her career working at various radio stations as an on-air talent as well as on-air television talent.

When not writing, Dee Dee can be found enjoying time with friends and family, diving into old novels, or watching a great basketball game. Her love for writing blossomed in childhood and has only grown stronger with each passing year. Dee Dee has spent years honing her craft, and her debut novel, *Love and Radio*, is a reflection of her lifelong journey as a writer.

With *Love and Radio*, Dee Dee Redding aims to create a world to which readers can escape and explore complex themes of the radio industry mingled with matters of the heart. Dee Dee is excited to continue writing and is currently working on another captivating novel for release in 2026.

Dee Dee Redding lives in Macon, GA, with two pets and can be found online **@deedeeredding.**

COMING SOON IN 2026:

Title: *Gun Point*
Teaser:

Prologue

I don't know when it happened exactly, but somewhere between closing one too many deals and filling out stacks of paperwork, I became … content. Content with my work, content with my solitude, and frankly, content with just keeping things simple.

I'm Angela Parkens, and by all accounts, I've built a life that most people would envy. I'm the senior business development director at Ocmulgee University Hospital in Macon, Georgia—proud of the position I've earned, the network I've built, and the many successes I've seen over the years. It's a job that requires all of me, all of my attention, and if I'm being honest, that's exactly how I like it. Selling my radio station, to the disappointment of my mother, afforded me the opportunity to take stock of my career path. So I decided I needed to make a change and the healthcare industry is where I landed. And after my marriage to James failed, I decided I wasn't going to let myself be a victim of circumstance. Sure, it wasn't easy letting go of fourteen years of marriage, but what's harder than that? Starting over. So, I threw myself into my career. I didn't have a choice, really. The kids were grown and out of the house—Kennedy is off in Atlanta at college, and Patrick . . . well, he's out there somewhere, doing his thing, but he doesn't come around much. That's the nature of being an "empty nester," I suppose. Once they're gone, the house is just . . . quieter.

It used to echo with their voices, with their chaos. Now, the silence is almost too loud. But I've learned to fill it. With work. With deadlines, meetings, and strategy sessions. These are the things that make sense to me. This is where I find my peace.

My friends, however, always remind me about the one thing I'm missing—the one thing they say I should be out looking for: *someone.*

"Angela, you need to get out more. You're too good to be alone," Naomi tells me every time we meet for our monthly wine nights. Her voice is always full of that well-meaning insistence, as if there's some magical formula for finding love in your early fifties. And Jen, always the practical one, is equally relentless.

"You can't spend your whole life focusing on work," she says, though it's usually followed by some casual mention of a new app or a "great guy" her friend met online. It's as if she thinks I'll just sign up for a dating site one day, like it's no big deal.

But the truth is, love terrifies me.

I've seen it all. The highs. The lows. The promises that break. When you've been married for as long as I was, and you've invested everything into that one person, you learn what it means to truly give yourself over to someone. And then, when it all unravels, you learn what it means to have it ripped away from you. I don't know if I have the energy or the heart to go through that again.

I've had my fair share of heartbreak—hell, haven't we all? But that last one? The one that made me say, *never again?* That one left a scar deeper than I ever imagined.

The thing is, I *do* miss companionship. I miss having someone to talk to at the end of a long day, someone to share a quiet moment with. But I'm not in a rush to jump back into something I'm not sure about. I've watched my girlfriends rush into relationships that were more about the comfort of having someone than the actual connection. I don't want to be one of them. Not again.

So, I focus on what I know. Work. The hospital. I'm good at it. I'm *great* at it. And I don't need to prove anything to anyone except myself.

But then there are nights like tonight, when I sit in the quiet of my home, the faint sound of traffic drifting through the window, and I can't help but wonder if maybe, just maybe, there's room in my life for something more. Something *outside* of my carefully constructed routine.

I don't know where that something is, or who it will be. But for now, it's easier to stay in my lane. Focus on the things that don't hurt. The things that don't leave you wondering if it's all worth it.

I suppose I'll let the universe decide when it's time for me to open up again. But I can't say I'm exactly looking for it. Maybe that's the way love should find you—when you least expect it.

For now, I'll keep doing what I do best—keeping everything under control. Even my heart.